THIS DIARY BELONGS TO:

Nikki J. Maxwell

PRIVATE & CONFIDENTIAL

If found, please return to ME for REWARD!

(NO SNOOPING ALLOWED!!!☹)

ALSO BY
Rachel Renée Russell

Dork Diaries:
Tales from a Not-So-Fabulous Life

Dork Diaries 2:
Tales from a Not-So-Popular Party Girl

Dork Diaries 3:
Tales from a Not-So-Talented Pop Star

Dork Diaries 3½:
How to Dork Your Diary

Dork Diaries 5:
Tales from a Not-So-Smart Miss Know-It-All

Dork Diaries 6:
Tales from a Not-So-Happy Heartbreaker

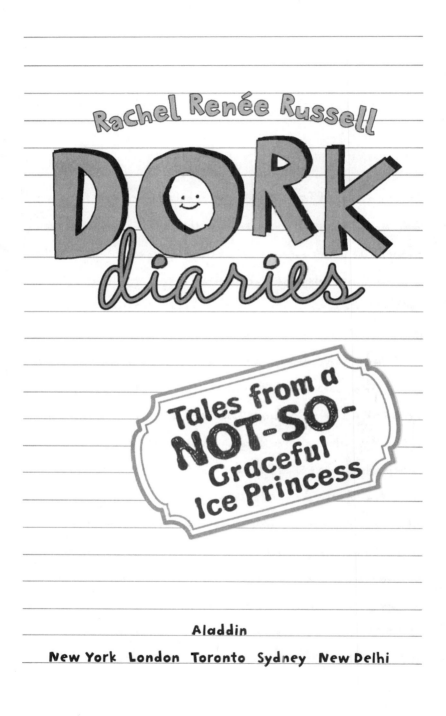

Rachel Renée Russell

DORK diaries

Tales from a NOT-SO- Graceful Ice Princess

Aladdin

New York   London   Toronto   Sydney   New Delhi

ALADDIN * An imprint of Simon & Schuster Children's Publishing Division * 1230 Avenue of the Americas, New York, NY 10020 * First Aladdin hardcover edition June 2012 * Copyright © 2012 by Rachel Renée Russell * All rights reserved, including the right of reproduction in whole or in part in any form. * ALADDIN is a trademark of Simon & Schuster, Inc., and related logo is a registered trademark of Simon & Schuster, Inc. * For information about special discounts for bulk purchases, please contact Simon & Schuster Special Sales at 1-866-506-1949 or business@simonandschuster.com. * The Simon & Schuster Speakers Bureau can bring authors to your live event. For more information or to book an event contact the Simon & Schuster Speakers Bureau at 1-866-248-3049 or visit our website at www.simonspeakers.com. * Designed by Lisa Vega * The text of this book was set in Skippy Sharp. * Manufactured in the United States of America 0613 FFG * 10 9 8 7   * Full CIP data for this book is available from the Library of Congress * ISBN 978-1-4424-1192-0 * ISBN 978-1-4424-1193-7 (eBook)

To my daughter Erin,
the original, slightly insecure Dork,
who grew up to be
a bold, brainy, and beautiful Dork

ACKNOWLEDGMENTS

To all of my Dork Diaries fans—thank you for allowing these books into your hearts. There could be no Nikki Maxwell without you. Why? Because YOU are HER! Stay uniquely you and always remember to let your inner DORK shine through.

Liesa Abrams Mignogna, my fabulous editor, who makes writing these books so inspiring and so much fun that I STILL pinch myself to make sure I'm not dreaming. Like Nikki Maxwell, you're an amazing real-life Dork with a hot photographer crush (your hubby!). Thank you for being my dream editor!

Lisa Vega, my supertalented art director, who works tirelessly on this book series and knows the Dork Diaries character art SO well you're able to tell ME when MacKenzie is having a bad hair day. That's just too awesomely weird.

Mara Anastas, Paul Crichton, Carolyn Swerdloff, Matt Pantoliano, Katherine Devendorf, Alyson Heller, and the rest of my wonderful team at Aladdin/Simon & Schuster, thank you for taking this series into the stratosphere with your vision and hard work.

Daniel Lazar, my supersweet, hardworking agent at

Writers House, thank you for your blood, sweat, and tears. There's just no way I could have done any of this without you. Most of all, thank you for supporting my dreams and slightly wacky ideas. You are truly a dear friend.

A special thanks to Stephen Barr for all your help on our *How to Dork Your Diary* book and for keeping me laughing. And to Torie Doherty for keeping everything organized and sending me those exciting e-mails.

Maja Nikolic, Cecilia de la Campa, and Angharad Kowal, my foreign rights agents at Writers House, thank you for putting the Dork Diaries books into the hands of children around the world.

Nikki Russell, my supertalented assistant artist, and Erin Russell, my supertalented assistant writer. OMG! Where do I begin? I am so happy and blessed to be your mom. Thank you for helping me bring this book series to the world. You're the original Dorks, who were (and still ARE) my inspiration for writing these books. I love you both SO much!

Sydney James, Cori James, Presli James, Arianna Robinson, and Mikayla Robinson, my nieces, for being brutal critique partners and willing to work for a shopping spree at the mall and cheese fries.

OMG!

I have never been so EMBARRASSED in my entire life!!

And this time, it WASN'T at the hands of my snobby, lip-gloss-addicted enemy, MacKenzie Hollister.

I still can't figure out why my very own sister, Brianna, would humiliate me like this.

It all started earlier this afternoon, when I noticed my hair was greasier than a supersized order of fries. I needed either a shower or an emergency Jiffy Lube oil change. I'm so NOT lying.

I hadn't been in the shower more than a minute when SOMEONE started pounding on the bathroom door like a maniac. I nervously peeked out of the shower and was like, "What the . . . ??!!"

"How much longer are you going to HOG the bathroom?" Brianna yelled. "NIKKI . . . ?!"

BAM!! BAM!! BAM!!

"Brianna, stop banging on the door! I'm in the shower!"

"But I think I left my doll in there. She and Miss Penelope were having a pool party and—"

"WHAT?! Sorry, Brianna! I do NOT want to hear about your poo in the potty."

"NO! I said 'POOL PARTY'! I need to come in and get my doll so I—"

"I CAN'T open the door right now. GO AWAY!!"

"But, Nikki, I gotta use the toilet! Really BAD!"

"Just use the one downstairs!"

"But my doll isn't in the bathroom downstairs!"

"Sorry, but you can't get your doll right now! Wait until I'm done with my shower!"

Unfortunately, one minute later . . .

NIKKI, OPEN THE DOOR! YOU HAVE A
PHONE CALL! NIKKI?!

4

"You need to open the door so you can talk on the phone!"

BAM!! BAM!! BAM!!

Did Brianna think I was stupid or something? I was NOT about to fall for the old open—the—bathroom—door—because—you—have—a—very—important—telephone—call trick.

"Sure, Brianna! Just tell 'em I don't feel like talking right now."

"Um, hello. Nikki says she doesn't want to talk right now. . . . I don't know? Hold on . . . ! Nikki, the person wants to know when to call back."

BAM!! BAM!! BAM!!

"NIKKI?! The person wants to know when—"

"NEVER! Tell them to call back NEVER! And they can DROP DEAD for all I care. All I want to do right now is TAKE A SHOWER!! So, please, Brianna! Just LEAVE ME ALONE!!"

"Um, hello. Nikki said to call her back never! And drop dead too! . . . Uh-huh. And guess why . . . ?!"

That's when it occurred to me that just maybe someone WAS actually on the telephone. But WHO? I hardly ever get any telephone calls.

"Because YOU got COOTIES! That's why!"

Brianna laughed like a criminally insane clown.

I was a little worried because that insult sounded really . . . familiar. She'd said the exact same thing to someone just yesterday. But there was no way that person would EVER call ME!

Suddenly I got this really sick, panicky feeling deep inside, and my mouth started screaming, "NOOOOOOOO!"

I grabbed a towel and scrambled out of the

shower soaking wet and completely covered in
soap suds.

"Okay, Brianna!!" I whisper-shouted. "GIVE. ME.
THAT. PHONE. *NOW!*"

But she just stuck her tongue out at me and
continued blabbing on the phone like she was talking
to a long-lost friend from kindergarten.

Nikki ALWAYS hogs the
bathroom! My mom yells at
her because she's so messy.
And when she wakes up
in the morning,
she looks
superscary.
But that's
because she has
hairy legs and
crusty eye boogers!

I could NOT believe
Brianna was telling all
of MY personal business
like that. How DARE
she?! "Brianna! Hand over that phone or else . . . !"

7

"Say 'pretty please with sugar on top'!"

"Okay! Give me the phone, pretty please with sugar on top!"

"NO! Too bad, so sad!" Then that evil little munchkin stuck her tongue out at me (AGAIN!) and continued blabbing on the phone.

"Anyway, my friend Miss Penelope sneaked Nikki's new perfume. She loved how it smelled even though she doesn't got a nose. We sprayed it on stuff to make it smell pretty. Like my feet, the garbage can in the garage, and that dead squirrel in Mrs. Wallabanger's backyard!"

Hijacking my phone calls was bad enough. But she's been fumigating things with my Sassy Sasha perfume as well?! I wanted to STRANGLE her!

"Give me that PHONE, you little BRAT!" I hissed.

But she just said "Toodles!" and took off running.

8

Chasing Brianna was VERY dangerous!

OMG! At one point I slipped and almost slid right down the stairs and into the kitchen. That would have been a first-degree rug burn for sure! OUCH! It made me cringe just thinking about it!

I finally cornered Brianna and was just about to tackle her, when she dropped the phone and ran screaming down the hall. "Help! Help! The slime mold in the shower grew arms and legs and is trying to SLIME me! Somebody call 911!"

I picked up the phone and tried to act coolly nonchalant, and not like I was standing there . . .

1. In a bath towel

2. Dripping wet, AND

3. Covered with enough soap suds to wash a small herd of very dirty llamas.

I cleared my throat and answered in my cutest, most perky-sounding voice . . .

"UM . . . HELLO-OO!!"

"Nikki? What's up! It's me, Brandon!"

I could NOT believe what my ears were actually hearing. This was the very FIRST time my crush had ever called me! I thought I was going to have a heart attack right there on the spot.

"Hi, Brandon! I'm really sorry. That was my little sister. She makes up the craziest stuff. Actually."

"No problem! So . . . I'm just calling to let you know I'm inviting a few friends over for my birthday in January. I was hoping you, Chloe, and Zoey would come."

That's when I fainted. Okay, ALMOST fainted.

"Wow! Um, well! I, er . . . Can you hold on for a minute? There's something I need to do."

"Sure. Do you want me to call you back?"

"Nope. It'll only take a minute."

I carefully covered the phone with my hand and then

proceeded to have a massively severe attack of RCS, also known as . . .

ROLLER COASTER SYNDROME!!

WHEEEE!

Okay. So maybe I overreacted just a little bit.

It wasn't like Brandon was asking me out on a date or something. I wish!

Anyway, after we finished our telephone conversation, I pinched myself really hard just to make sure I wasn't dreaming. OUCH!! Yep, I was awake! Which means CHLOE, ZOEY, AND I ARE INVITED TO BRANDON'S PARTY ☺!!!

It's gonna be a blast! I can hardly wait!

Especially considering the fact that I'm the biggest dork at my school and pretty much NEVER get invited to parties.

OMG! I JUST HAD THE MOST HORRIBLE THOUGHT ☹!!! . . .

After his conversation with Brianna, Brandon probably thinks I'm some kind of, um . . .

HAIRY-LEGGED . . .

CRUSTY-EYED . . .

FREAK!!!

Why would he want to hang out with ME?!!

There is NO WAY I can go to Brandon's party!

I'm going to call him back right now and tell him I can't come.

DUH!! I completely forgot! I STILL need to finish my SHOWER! So I'll call him afterward.

And then I'm going to crawl into a very deep hole and . . . DIE of EMBARRASSMENT!

☹!

I'm totally dreading seeing Brandon in school today.

It's hard to believe that just a couple days ago we were rocking our school's talent show together in our band, Dorkalicious (also known as Actually, I'm Not Really Sure Yet). Yes, it's a crazy name and a long story.

He even gave me lessons on his drum set. It seemed like we were FINALLY becoming good friends.

But then Brianna the Brat RUINED everything!

I'm surprised Brandon even bothered to invite me to his party. I bet he only did it because he feels sorry for me or something.

I wanted to talk to Chloe and Zoey about all of this during gym, but I didn't get a chance to. Mainly because the entire class was buzzing about nabbing a really cool, FREE T-shirt for this show called Holiday on Ice.

But after our gym teacher practically shattered my eardrums, all I really wanted was for her to accidentally SWALLOW that stupid whistle!

Then she made a big announcement. . . .

"Okay. Listen up, people! We'll be starting our ice-skating section next week. Grades will be based on the skill level each student successfully masters. However, as part of our Westchester Country Day holiday tradition and to encourage community service, all eighth-grade students participating in the Westchester *Holiday on Ice* charity show on December thirty-first will get to practice their routines during class and receive an automatic A. Yes, folks! You heard that right! I'll be giving out As like candy canes to support this great cause. Just let me know whether you'll be doing the skills testing or the ice show. Now hustle up to the table and grab a free *Holiday on Ice* T-shirt. Then get started on your warm-up exercises."

That T-shirt thing did *NOT* go so well for me.

By the time I got to the table, all that was left was size XXXXXL. MacKenzie, of course, looked like she was ready for the summer cover of *Seventeen* magazine.

MACKENZIE, LOOKING CUTE AND
TRENDY IN HER NEW T-SHIRT

ME, LOOKING LIKE AN UGLY, SHAPELESS BLOB

I was so . . . DISGUSTED ☹!

Of course MacKenzie took one look at my T-shirt and started giving me unwanted fashion advice. "Nikki, do you want to hear my idea for how to make your T-shirt stylishly elegant, yet practical?"

"No, MacKenzie. Actually, I don't."

"Just add three inches of white lace around the hem, a veil, and a bouquet of flowers, and you can use it as a WEDDING dress! Then all you have to do is PAY some FREAKISHLY ugly guy to marry you!"

I could NOT believe she actually said that right to my face like that.

"Thanks, MacKenzie!" I said, smiling sweetly. "But where will I find a freakishly ugly guy? Oh, I know! Do YOU have a twin BROTHER?!"

Only MacKenzie would be STUPID enough to make a wedding dress out of a five-sizes-too-big T-shirt. But that's because her IQ is LOWER than an empty bottle of nail polish!

MACKENZIE'S VERY STUPID IDEA FOR A DESIGNER T-SHIRT WEDDING DRESS

ME → ← VEIL

BRIDAL BOUQUET

XXXXXL T-SHIRT

← LACE AT HEM

SUPERCUTE SHOES →

Calling MacKenzie a "mean girl" is an understatement. She's a GRIZZLY BEAR with a French manicure and blond hair extensions.

But I'm not jealous of her or anything. Like, how juvenile would THAT be?

Anyway, I was excited about skating in class. The last time I did it was back in, like, third grade, and it was a lot of fun.

Chloe said we'd be skating at the ice hockey arena at WCD High School.

Apparently, the *Holiday on Ice* show is a big deal, and only students in grades eight to twelve can participate to raise money for their favorite charity. The show donates $3,000 to every charity that a skater, skating pair, or group sponsors.

We were about to start our exercises when suddenly Chloe got this crazy look in her eyes and started doing jazz hands.

"Hey, you guys! Guess what I'm thinking!"

But I already knew. Lately, she's been obsessed with this new book called *The Ice Princess*.

It's about a girl and a guy who have been best friends since grade school.

She's training to be a world-class figure skater

while he's working toward a spot on the Olympic hockey team.

Just as they're about to fall in love, they discover that their ice arena is the secret hideout of the Deadly Ice Vambies, half-vampire and half-zombie beings whose supernatural ice-skating abilities grow more and more powerful every time they eat a double bacon cheeseburger.

"There is no reason why WE can't be Ice Princesses too! Just like Crystal Coldstone!" Chloe sighed dreamily.

Personally, I could think of TWO very good reasons why we COULDN'T be like Crystal.

First, we haven't been training with a skating coach for the past twelve years. Second, it was going to be really difficult to slay Deadly Ice Vambies on school nights and still get our homework done on time.

Zoey got this wistful, faraway look in her eyes.

"How ROMANTIC! And hockey players ARE kind of cute! Besides, I'd much rather make up a really cool skating routine and get an A than do boring skills testing. We'll have a blast! How about it, Nikki?"

"I don't know, guys. Skating for a charity is a really big responsibility. They're going to be depending on us for money to help keep their doors open. And what if something goes wrong?"

"Come on, Nikki!" Chloe whined. "We're not good enough to skate individually, and skating pairs require a girl and a guy. But the three of us can skate as a group. We can't do this without you!"

"Sorry, but you're going to have to find someone else!" I said, shaking my head.

"But we want YOU!" Zoey pleaded.

"Yeah, and don't forget! We were there for you when you needed us for the talent show," Chloe argued. "BFFs help each other!"

Okay, I have to admit Chloe had a good point about the talent show. But it wasn't like I'd promised them my firstborn child in exchange for them singing backup.

Then Chloe and Zoey shrewdly resorted to a sophisticated tactic that effectively rendered me helpless. . . .

PLEASE, PLEASE, PLEASE, PLEASE
PLEASE, PLEASE, PLEASE, PLEASE!!

BEGGING!!!

"Okay, guys! I'm IN! But you can't say I didn't warn you!" I sighed.

We sealed the deal with a group hug.

"Great! Now all we have to do is find a local charity to skate for," Zoey said.

"Unfortunately, that's going to be the hardest part," Chloe said. "All of the high school kids have been signing up charities for a few weeks now. So we're getting a really late start. But I'm pretty sure we'll find one," she added cheerfully.

"OMG!" Zoey squealed. "This will be just like our old *Ballet of the Zombies* days! Only we'll be getting an A instead of a D."

Actually, I kind of like that part too. It is going to be great to finally get an A in gym ☺!

Fortunately, ice-skating DOESN'T involve embarrassing armpit stains, painful stomach cramps, or getting whacked in the head by a ball, like most of the stuff we are forced to do in gym.

And all of our work is going to be for a really great cause that will help the community.

But most important, I'll be making Chloe and Zoey superhappy by allowing them to live out their dreams.

We decided to skate to "Dance of the Sugar Plum Fairy" since it has a holiday theme. And we figured being fairy princesses would be superexciting and glamorous.

So I'm not going to stress out about this whole *Holiday on Ice* thing.

As long as I have my two BFFs by my side, everything is going to work out just fine.

I mean, how HARD can figure skating be?!

☺!!

Today in social studies we discussed career goals.

But since I plan to attend a major university to become a professional illustrator, I decided to spend the hour writing in my diary instead.

I felt it was the right thing to do since teachers always nag us students to use our class time wisely.

Most of the kids had not given much thought to their futures.

But my friend Theodore Swagmire III was totally obsessing over it.

And it didn't help that the class snickered when he shared his plans for the future. I felt a little sorry for him. He's one of the dorkiest guys in the school.

So, being the very kind and supportive friend that I am, I decided to encourage Theo to pursue his goals in life:

The GOOD news is that our little chat made Theo feel a lot better ☺!!

The BAD news is that he decided to start saving his allowance to buy a magic wand ☹!

Anyway, after class was over, Theo asked me if I was planning to come to Brandon's party in January. I wanted to tell the truth and just say no.

But instead, I made up an excuse. And not just a run-of-the-mill flimsy excuse. It was a totally unbelievable, embarrassingly STUPID one.

"I was planning to come. But I found out I had, um . . . an appointment to . . . take my sick . . . um, unicorn . . . to the . . . vet, actually."

Theo looked superconfused and scratched his head. "You have a unicorn?"

I wanted to say, "Hey, Wizard Boy! I probably got MY unicorn from the same place you're getting YOUR magic wand!" But I didn't.

Then in biology class, my very cruddy day turned into a complete DISASTER!

Brandon and I said hi to each other, but that was about it. The entire hour he just kind of stared at me with this perplexed look on his face.

He was probably imagining me as some kind of
CRUSTY-EYED, HAIRY-LEGGED BEAST!

← ME

MacKenzie took full advantage of the situation and would NOT shut up!

I almost PUKED on my lab report when I heard her ask Brandon if he thought her Berry-Sweet-'n'-Flirty lip gloss color matched her flawless complexion.

I could not believe she actually had the nerve to ask him something so ridiculously VAIN.

Especially when EVERYONE knows MacKenzie's so-called flawless complexion is from U-PAY-WE-SPRAY Tanning Salon at the mall.

That pukey-orange tan they sprayed on her is so tacky. Personally, I think she looks like a sunburned Malibu Barbie dipped in Cheetos dust.

Then MacKenzie got all giggly and said, "Oh, by the way, Brandon, I heard you're having a party."

I was like, "Yeah, MacKenzie! And you'll ONLY be HEARING about it, because you're NOT invited!"

But I just said that inside my head, so no one else heard it but me.

I was shocked by what that girl did next!

She tried to HYPNOTIZE Brandon into inviting her to his party by flirting with him and twirling her hair AROUND and AROUND and AROUND her finger.

Just watching her made ME dizzy.

Thank goodness our teacher interrupted her. "MacKenzie, if you have time to chitchat in class, please go to the back of the room and clean out all of the rat cages. Otherwise, PLEASE. SIT. DOWN!"

MacKenzie practically RAN back to her seat.

OMG! It was SO funny! She totally deserved it.

But now she's giving ME the EVIL EYE from across the room like it was MY fault she almost got stuck doing rat-poop duty.

Anyway, I'm still convinced Brandon gave me a pity invitation. He probably didn't want to hurt my feelings.

I plan to tell him tomorrow that I can't make it to his party because I have another activity planned for that exact same time.

WHAT will I be doing?

Sitting on my bed in my pajamas, STARING at the wall and SULKING!!!!!!! ☹!!

←ME

This morning I was feeling kind of down.

Even Chloe and Zoey noticed and asked me if I was okay. But I decided NOT to tell them about my mega-embarrassing phone conversation with Brandon. Especially after they went on and on about how EXCITED they were about his party.

On my way to lunch I decided to stop by my locker and drop off my backpack.

I was beyond surprised when I opened my locker door and a NOTE fell out!

At first I thought it was from Chloe and Zoey and they were trying to cheer me up or something.

But then I read it. Like, THREE TIMES!

OMG! I thought I was going to have a meltdown right there in front of my locker. . . .

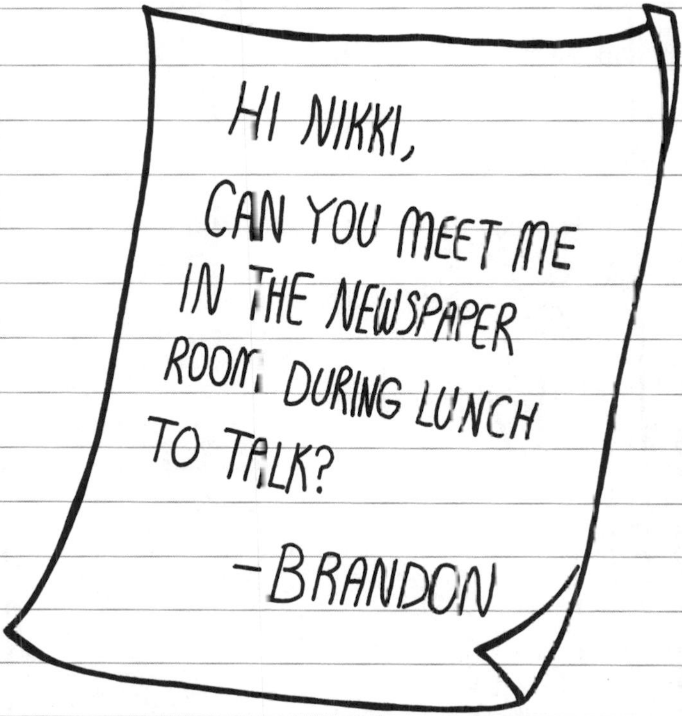
HI NIKKI,
CAN YOU MEET ME IN THE NEWSPAPER ROOM DURING LUNCH TO TALK?
-BRANDON

I had no idea what Brandon wanted to talk to me about.

My heart was pounding as I peeked inside the newspaper room. I immediately recognized his shaggy hair behind a computer monitor.

"Nikki!" Brandon smiled, waved, and gestured for me to come over.

Like an idiot, I looked behind me to make sure he wasn't talking to some other, um . . . Nikki.

HI, BRANDON. DID YOU WANT TO TALK TO ME ABOUT SOMETHING?

"Yeah. Actually, I do." That's when I noticed Brandon looked a little nervous too.

"Well! HERE I AM!" I blurted out all cheerful-like and louder than I meant to.

"Okay, um, I talked to Theo yesterday, and he said you can't come to my party."

GULP!

Brandon talked to . . . THEO?!

OH! CRUD!

I just kept smiling stupidly as Brandon continued. "He said something about you having to take care of a, um, sick unicorn?"

Just great! NOW Brandon was going to think I am a crusty-eyed, hairy-legged, SCHIZOPHRENIC HYPOCHONDRIAC!

"Really? Theo told you that?" I blinked my eyes all

innocentlike and laughed nervously. "That's . . . quite hilarious, actually. Theo's got a big imagination. Just like my little sister. She's as cute a button, but you can't believe a word she says. Especially if it's about . . . ME!"

"Yeah, tell me about it." Brandon laughed. "I wish I had a dollar for every time Brianna told me I have cooties." Suddenly he stared at me so intensely it made me squirm. "Nikki, you didn't seriously think I actually believed any of that stuff Brianna said about you, did you?"

"OMG! Of course not! Like, how immature would THAT be?" I giggled nervously. "Actually, Chloe, Zoey, and I can't WAIT to come to your party."

Brandon broke into a big grin. "Cool! You had me worried there for a minute."

"So, what are you working on right now?" I asked, trying to change the topic.

I leaned over and peeked at his computer screen.

I saw snapshots of the cutest puppy and kitten.

"AWWW!" I gushed. "They're ADORABLE!"

"Those two are from the Fuzzy Friends Animal Rescue Center. These pictures are going to run in the *Westchester Herald* next week."

"Wow! Impressive. Does the animal center pay you to do that?"

"Nope. I guess you could say I volunteer my time. I want to be a veterinarian one day, so I really enjoy working with animals. Even though photographing them can be pretty challenging."

"Well, I think it's great that you take the time to help out. Sounds like fun!"

"It is. Hey! Why don't you come volunteer with me on Friday? I could use your help."

"Okay! That would be VERY cool!"

Brandon brushed his bangs out of his eyes and gave me a crooked smile.

I suddenly felt very nervous, giddy, and . . . nauseous.

That's when he kind of stared at me and I stared back at him.

Then we both smiled and blushed.

All of this staring, smiling, and blushing seemed to go on, like, FOREVER!

Brandon and I spent the rest of the lunch hour just hanging out and talking about the animal shelter.

He said it was run by a really nice semi—retired couple who used to own a pet shop.

Then he took some photos out of his backpack and showed me all the animals that had already been placed in homes.

So, not only is Brandon a supertalented photographer, but he has a really BIG heart, too.

And get this! We went to my locker to pick up my books, and then we walked to bio together!

SQUEEE!!!

MacKenzie kept glaring at me and whispering to Jessica the entire hour, but I just ignored her.

Okay, I admit it. I was wrong about the whole pity-invitation thing and Brandon not wanting to hang out with me.

I'm actually looking forward to going to his party.

And on Friday we're going to have a BLAST volunteering at Fuzzy Friends!!

Eat your heart out, MacKenzie!! ☺!!

During library today Chloe and Zoey were busy making telephone calls trying to find a charity for the *Holiday on Ice* show.

Chloe called nine places and Zoey called seven, but no luck.

The deadline for entering is next week, and we're not even CLOSE to finding a charity.

But there's even MORE bad news!

I just found out today that MacKenzie is also planning to participate in the *Holiday on Ice* show ☹!!

Why am I NOT surprised?!

Probably because she really IS a coldhearted Ice Princess! Okay, so maybe that nasty little comment ISN'T quite true.

Her heart isn't COLD! She DOESN'T have one!!

MACKENZIE AS A HEARTLESS ICE PRINCESS

While I was at my locker, I overheard MacKenzie
bragging to some CCPs (Cute, Cool & Popular kids)

that she's been taking figure skating lessons since she was seven years old and plans to skate to music from Swan Lake.

But this is the crazy part. She said she has FIVE charities BEGGING her to skate for them.

Can you believe THAT?! We're having trouble finding just one.

Although, now that I think about it, she was probably just saying all that stuff to impress everyone.

MacKenzie is SUCH a pathological liar! And a major DRAMA QUEEN.

I know it's supposed to be for a good cause. But I'm starting to get a really BAD feeling about this Holiday on Ice thing.

I could hardly wait for school to be over. Every class just seemed to drag on and on and on. After the final bell rang, I rushed to my locker and Brandon was already there waiting for me.

"Ready to go?" he said, smiling.

"Yep! Oh, wait! I have a present for you from Brianna," I said, digging into my backpack.

Brandon pretended to be frightened. "Brianna?! I don't know if I want it," he teased. "She says I have cooties. I don't think she likes me."

"She does. Well . . . actually, she doesn't!" I giggled. "But she wanted you to have this."

I handed Brandon about two yards of red satin ribbon, and he looked a little confused. Then he playfully tied it around his head.

"Oooh! Just the look I was going for!" he joked. "Tell Brianna I plan to wear it every day."

BRANDON, TOTALLY CRACKING ME UP WITH HIS WICKED SENSE OF HUMOR

I laughed really hard. "It's not for you, silly. It's for the animals. Brianna said if we tie bows around their necks, they'll look like presents. And since everyone loves a present, they'll find new homes really fast."

"The kid's a genius! Why didn't I think of that?"

I was a nervous wreck as we walked the four blocks to the Fuzzy Friends building. But Brandon kept me laughing the entire time.

Three new puppies had come in, and each one needed to be photographed.

They were absolutely adorable and playfully nibbled on my fingers.

I cut the ribbon into three pieces and tied them around their necks.

"Have a seat on the rug and hold the first puppy in your lap," Brandon instructed. "Your sweater will be the perfect background for a close-up."

THE PUPPY AND I BOTH SMILE
FOR THE CAMERA!

We finished up in about forty-five minutes, and Brandon placed the last puppy back in the cage.

I was a little sad when I went over to say good-bye to them. I especially liked the smallest one, which had a little circle around one eye. He barked and wagged his tail at me as if to say, "Please, don't go!"

But it felt really good knowing I was doing something to help them all find a new home.

I was just about to leave when the smallest puppy pressed his nose against the cage door and it swung open.

"HEY!" I said, surprised. "How did you—"

But before I could finish my sentence, he quickly jumped into my lap, knocking me off balance.

The other two puppies scampered close behind and pounced.

"WHOA!" I yelled as I fell over backward on the floor.

"Brandon! Help! The puppies got loose!" I giggled as they tickled my neck and chin.

But that guy was no help WHATSOEVER.

Not only was he LAUGHING at me, he just stood there taking pictures.

His camera sounded like he was at a photo shoot for Fashion Week or something. *Chick-koo. Chick-koo. Chick-koo. Chick-koo.*

"My bad!" he said, grinning. "I guess I closed the cage but didn't latch it. Smile and say 'CHEESE!'"

"Brandon! I'm going to . . . KILL you!" I laughed as I tried unsuccessfully to herd the wiggly puppies back into the cage.

We finished up and walked back to school. Then I called my mom to come pick me up.

While we were waiting, Brandon made a very special thank-you card for Brianna. . . .

Those little pups looked SO SWEET in that photo!

I just knew Brianna was going to LOVE it!

And that red ribbon was perfect. I couldn't decide who wore it better, Brandon or the puppies.

Then Brandon totally surprised me and printed some of the snapshots he'd taken during the GREAT PUPPY ESCAPE. . . .

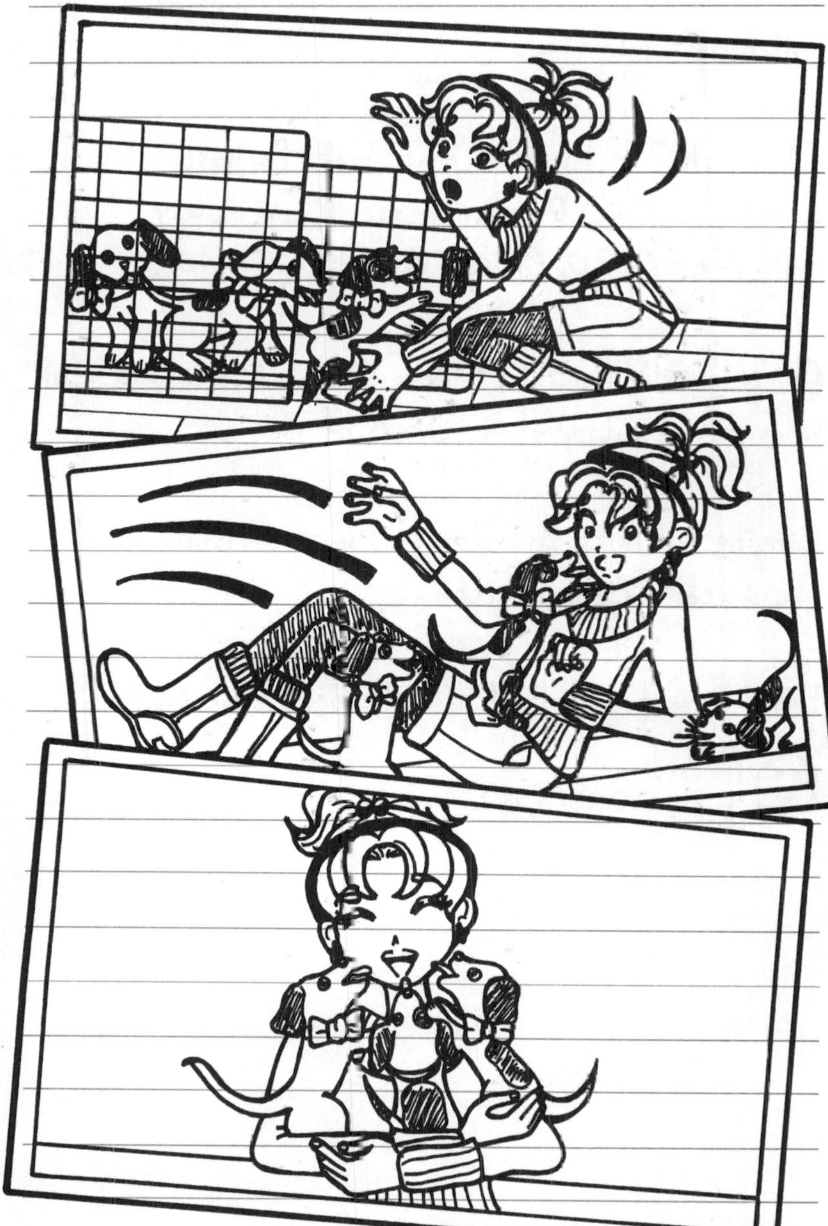

I couldn't believe I had actually lost my balance and fallen over like that.

OMG! What if Brandon now thinks I'm just a big, clumsy . . . OX?! Or even worse, a big, clumsy . . . HAIRY-LEGGED, CRUSTY-EYED . . . ox?!

Okay, I really need to take a CHILL PILL and stop worrying about what he thinks of me.

Hanging out with Brandon at Fuzzy Friends wasn't like a real date or anything.

But I have to admit, I had the best time EVER!

☺!

It's hard to believe that the holidays are right around the corner.

Mom and I spent most of the morning decorating our fake Christmas tree.

Dad and Brianna were busy outside working on what they called a "super-duper secret project."

Dad said their big surprise was going to:

1. Spread holiday cheer.

2. Be a source of great pride for our family, AND

3. Drastically INCREASE our household income.

But I was hoping he'd surprise us with something more practical.

Like a NEW JOB!

One that does NOT involve him:

1. Working at MY school.

2. Driving a crazy-looking van with a roach on it.

3. Exterminating bugs.

4. Damaging my already very shabby reputation.

Finally, Dad and Brianna called us outside to see their surprise.

I had a really BAD feeling about their little project even before I actually saw what they had done. Mostly because Dad and Brianna have the combined IQ of a TOOTHBRUSH.

And I was right!

I took one look at their monstrosity and totally

FREAKED. . . .

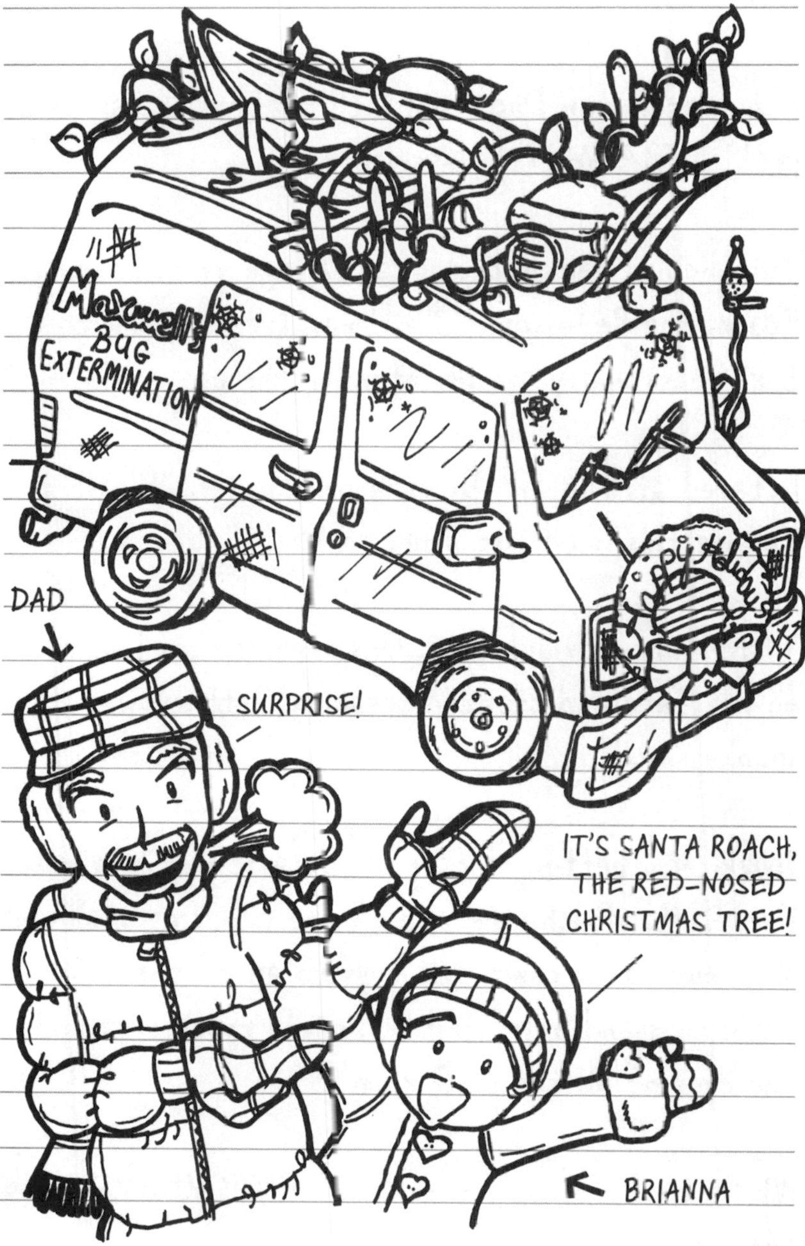
Maxwell's
BUG
EXTERMINATION
DAD
SURPRISE!
IT'S SANTA ROACH,
THE RED-NOSED
CHRISTMAS TREE!
BRIANNA

I was like, WHAT is THAT?!

Riding around in Dad's van with that roach can be a pretty TRAUMATIC experience.

But undoing the psychological damage from Santa Roach, the Red-Nosed Christmas Tree is going to take years and years of intensive therapy.

I stared at Dad and Brianna in disbelief. "Please! Tell me this is all just a big PRANK?!"

That's when Brianna got this superserious look on her face and started speaking in this low, spooky voice.

"Nikki, you better be careful! Because on Christmas Eve, Santa Roach rises out of the pumpkin patch and gives out candy canes and toys to all of the good little girls and boys! And he squirts roach spray into the eyes of all the BAD kids."

Which, by the way, is the MOST RIDICULOUS thing I've ever heard!!

Brianna must think I'm an IDIOT!! I know her little story is just a rip-off of another well-known legend.

But just in case any of that stuff she said about the roach spray is true, I'm going to start sleeping with my sunglasses on.

Anyway, this weekend I was seriously planning to come clean and tell Chloe and Zoey about my WCD scholarship and my dad being the school exterminator and all.

I'm just SO sick of all the decept on and lies.

I had no doubt WHATSOEVER that Chloe and Zoey were my TRUE friends and would accept me for who I really am.

But that was BEFORE Santa Roach became a part of my STINKIN' family!!

There's just NO WAY I can tell my BFFs now!

☹!!

I was really surprised when I got up this morning and looked out the window. We had a really big snowstorm late last night and got, like, six inches of snow.

My dad usually hates big snows. But today he was superexcited to go outside to clear the driveway.

Earlier in the fall he bought this rusty old snowblower at a yard sale.

Dad is always buying dangerous pieces of junk from yard sales. I'll never forget the time he took us out on the lake in an old canoe with no paddles. If we hadn't gotten rescued by that coast guard helicopter, we probably would have drowned.

Dad insisted that he got a real bargain because a brand-new snowblower costs around $300 and he paid only $20 for his.

Well, now we all know why his snowblower was so

cheap. The snow-chute thingy was rusted and permanently stuck in one position. . . .

DAD, TRYING TO CLEAR OUR DRIVEWAY WITH HIS BROKEN SNOWBLOWER

That busted snowblower kept blowing snow right back onto the area Dad had just cleared. He couldn't figure out what he was doing wrong.

Poor Dad was out in the snow trying to clear the driveway for three hours. Mom had to go out there and drag him back into the house before his body parts froze solid.

I actually felt sorry for him. And Mom did too, because she went right online and ordered Dad a brand—new snowblower.

The bad news is that our driveway STILL needs to be dug out.

I explained to Mom I was willing to make a huge personal sacrifice and stay home from school for the next week or two until the new snowblower arrives.

But she just handed me a snow shovel and told me if I started shoveling right now, I'd have the driveway cleared out so I could go to school tomorrow morning.

Mom obviously had no appreciation for the tremendous sacrifice I was willing to make.

Today in English, our teacher reminded us that our *Moby-Dick* report is due in nine days. We were supposed to start reading the novel back in October, but I've been very busy with other stuff.

It's about a humongous whale and this crusty old sailor who has a purse and a really bad attitude. I'm so NOT lying!

Like most people, I assumed that Moby Dick was the captain's name or something. But it was actually the whale's name. Like, WHO in their right mind would name a whale Moby Dick?!

Our report is supposed to be about why the captain and the whale were mortal enemies. But to save time, I'm thinking about just skipping the book and writing the paper.

Hey, you don't have to be a literary scholar (or read the book) to know WHY that whale was probably trying to kill that guy. . . .

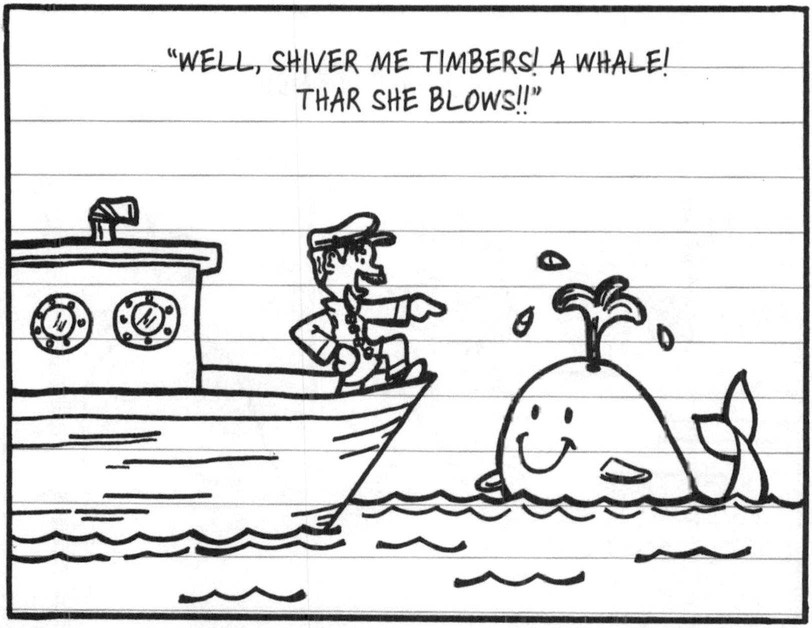
"WELL, SHIVER ME TIMBERS! A WHALE!
THAR SHE BLOWS!!"

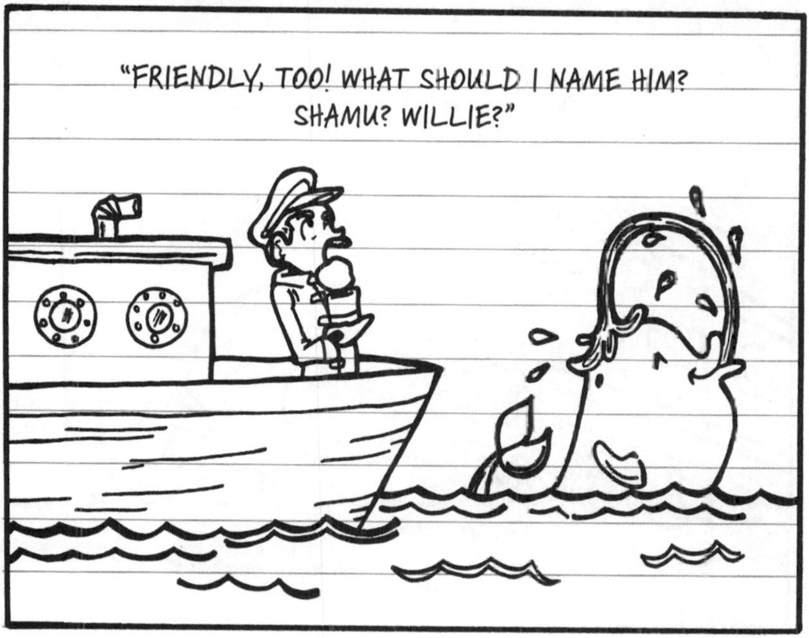
"FRIENDLY, TOO! WHAT SHOULD I NAME HIM?
SHAMU? WILLIE?"

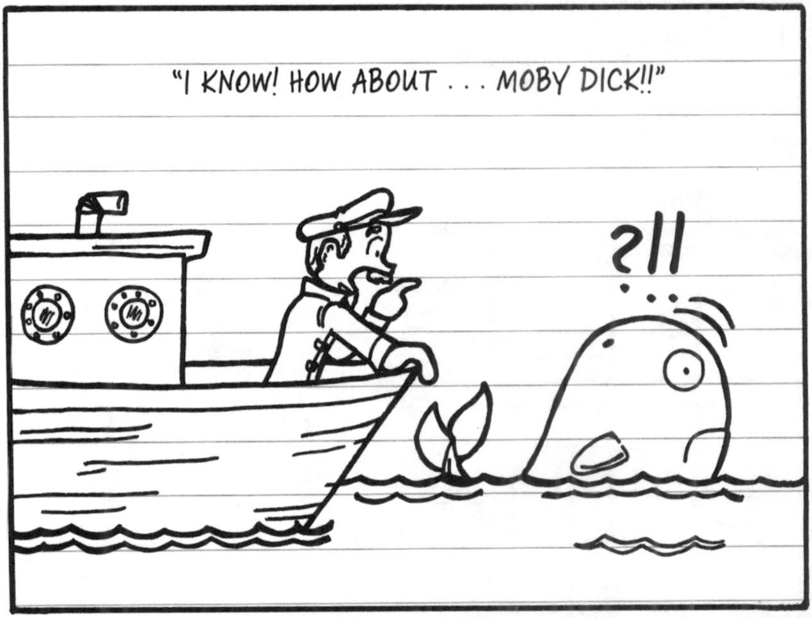
"I KNOW! HOW ABOUT . . . MOBY DICK!!"
?!!

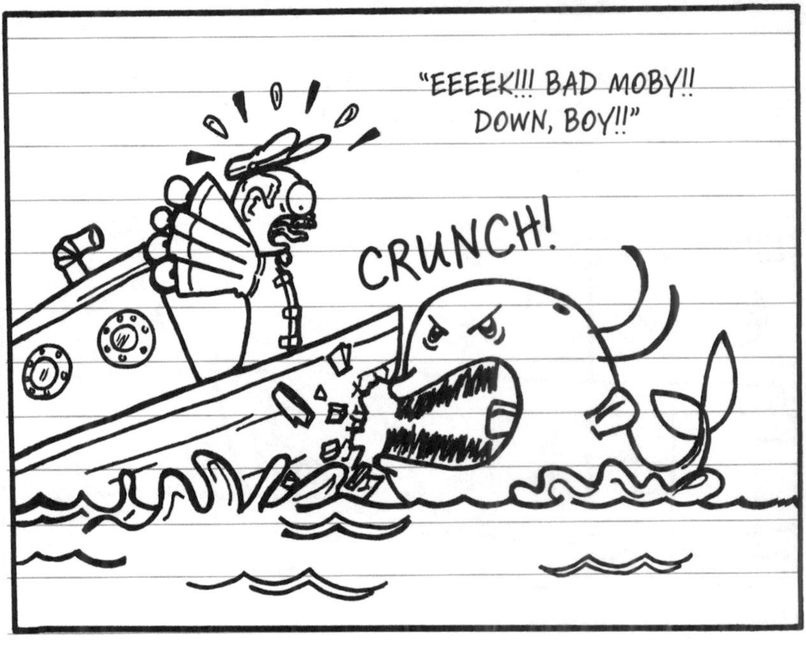
"EEEEK!!! BAD MOBY!!
DOWN, BOY!!"
CRUNCH!

Hey, if my mom had named ME Moby Dick, I would have been massively ticked off about it too.

I think dusty old classics like these should come with a sticker on the cover that says:

WARNING

READING THIS BOOK CAN BE HAZARDOUS TO YOUR HEALTH!

WHY?! Because *Moby-Dick* was so ridiculously BORING, I accidentally fell asleep, smacked my head on my desk, and darn near got a concussion!! . . .

OMG! I had this big purplish bruise right in the middle of my forehead.

And I'd only gotten to the SECOND sentence!

As an additional precaution, I think students should be required to wear protective headgear while reading books like *Moby-Dick*.

Tomorrow I'm going to wear my bike helmet to class to protect against further head injuries.

Even though I was bummed about that paper being due next week, I was really looking forward to seeing Brandon today.

I wanted to tell him what a great time I had hanging out at Fuzzy Friends. And that I thought he'd make a great veterinarian one day.

But unfortunately, I didn't see him at lunch and he wasn't in bio.

It was the weirdest coincidence that while I was in the girls' bathroom, I overheard Jessica and MacKenzie gossiping about Brandon.

Jessica said he had been called down to the office during first period and he'd left school for an important family matter. Well, that explained everything.

And get this! MacKenzie said it's rumored that Brandon's dad is a wealthy U.S. diplomat at the French embassy and his mom is French royalty.

Apparently, his family lived in Paris for ten years, but he never talks about it because he probably wants to keep the fact that he's a prince or something a big secret. And that's why Brandon is fluent in French.

Then MacKenzie told Jessica that since she's an office assistant, she should check Brandon's school records to see if all those rumors are true.

But Jessica said she doesn't have access to certain information because it's kept on a special computer in the principal's office.

I was both shocked and appalled that those girls were actually talking about snooping in highly confidential student records.

It wasn't like I was eavesdropping on their very private conversation or anything. I was in that bathroom stall totally minding my own business.

I just happened to feel like climbing up on the toilet seat, standing on my tippy toes, and peeking over the top. To get, you know, some fresh air!

MACKENZIE AND JESSICA, GOSSIPING
ABOUT BRANDON

I just hope everything is okay with Brandon. I'm guessing he probably had a dentist appointment or something.

Jessica and MacKenzie are always sticking their noses in other people's business!

They are so PATHETIC!

But what if Brandon REALLY IS secretly a prince or something?!! He IS in Honors French!

OMG!!! SQUEEEEEE!!

☺!!

TUESDAY, DECEMBER 10

I'm kind of in SHOCK right now ☹!!

Brandon just left my locker about thirty minutes ago. I could tell right away that something was really bothering him.

He gave me the rest of the photos he'd taken of me during the Great Puppy Escape and thanked me for helping him.

But when I mentioned how much fun I'd had and that I wanted to volunteer on a regular basis, he just looked really sad and stared at the floor.

Brandon explained that he'd just gotten very bad news from Phil and Betty Smith, the owners of Fuzzy Friends. Phil broke his leg and is going to be in the hospital in traction for the next two months.

Unfortunately, there is no way Betty can keep the shelter open without his help.

BRANDON TELLS ME THE SAD NEWS
ABOUT FUZZY FRIENDS

As soon as Betty finds a place that will accept the eighteen cats and dogs in her shelter, she plans to sell the building to the flower shop next door.

No wonder Brandon was so upset. Starting tomorrow, he plans to spend every day after school helping to care for the animals until they all get transferred or placed in new homes.

I feel really bad for him. Mainly because I know how much he loves that place.

I mentioned all of this to Chloe and Zoey in gym class, and we had a deep discussion during sit-ups about how we could possibly help.

That's when I came up with the brilliant idea of Chloe, Zoey, and me skating in the *Holiday on Ice* show to raise money for Fuzzy Friends!

Of course my BFFs were superhappy about us FINALLY finding a charity. They also said it's the perfect opportunity for ME to show Brandon what a good friend I am. Then Zoey said . . .

I just kind of smiled at Zoey and nodded.

But to be honest, I didn't have the slightest idea WHAT she was talking about! Her comment had

NOTHING whatsoever to do with ANYTHING we were discussing!

Zoey is supersmart and I love her to death. But sometimes I wonder where she gets all of that cornball stuff.

Anyway, I agreed to discuss the *Holiday on Ice* idea with Brandon. We need a charity to skate for, and Fuzzy Friends needs the money to hire a part-time worker to replace Phil while he's recovering.

Zoey did the math and calculated that the $3,000 donation from *Holiday on Ice* would probably be enough to pay a worker for about two months.

I just hope Brandon thinks all of this is a good idea.

I didn't want to mention it to Chloe and Zoey, but I'm really worried we might have a little competition for Fuzzy Friends from someone else.

While Brandon was talking to me at my locker, I

couldn't help but notice MacKenzie slinking around, pretending to be putting on lip gloss.

PUH-LEEZE! She could have put on twenty-seven layers of lip gloss during the time she was eavesdropping on our very private conversation.

That girl is a SNAKE and will stop at nothing to get what she wants.

I just hope she already has a charity, like she has been bragging to her CCP friends.

Because if she DOESN'T . . . ?!

Things are going to get really UGLY!

☹!!

WEDNESDAY, DECEMBER II

Right now I'm so MAD at MacKenzie I could just . . . SPIT!!

My suspicions were correct! According to the gossip around school, MacKenzie is skating for Fuzzy Friends!

YES! FUZZY FRIENDS!!! I was like, NO!! WAY!!

I can't believe MacKenzie is actually trying to steal MY charity from right under my nose like this. I came up with that idea first, and she knows it. But I'm not going down without a fight!

When I saw her at her locker just now, she had the nerve to act all sweet and innocent. She even complimented my new sweater. Kind of.

She was all like, "Nikki! What a CUTE sweater! It's the PERFECT look! For a DOG. My poodle would LOVE it!"

MY SWEATER ☹

That girl is a charity-stealing BACKSTABBER!

I finally tracked Brandon down in the newspaper room during lunch. He had photos of all the animals at Fuzzy Friends and was busy typing up descriptions.

He explained that Betty is doubling her efforts to try to get all of her animals adopted before the shelter closes at the end of the month.

"OMG!" I exclaimed. "So soon?!"

I wanted to tell him about our plan to try to earn money for the shelter through the *Holiday on Ice* show.

But Brandon looked so down in the dumps. The last thing I wanted to do was set him up for another big disappointment.

Running that shelter was probably a lot of work. And it was very possible Betty just wanted to sell the building, collect the cash, retire to sunny Florida, and play bingo every day for the rest of her life.

If she turned down our offer to help keep the shelter open, Brandon would just be more miserable than ever. I felt SO sorry for him.

"Is there anything I can do to help?" I asked.

Brandon looked up at me, and his face immediately brightened.

"Yeah, you can put these photos in order based on the ad numbers. Thanks! And no matter what happens, I just want you to know that I'll never forget you . . ." He nervously brushed his bangs out of his eyes and continued awkwardly. "Helping me with all of this stuff, I mean."

I was a little surprised he was so . . . serious. I tried to lighten the mood. "Hey, that's what friends are for. Even though YOU GOT COOTIES, DUDE!"

We both laughed really hard at my wacky impression of Brianna. Then we both kind of blushed and smiled at each other. All of this laughing, blushing, and smiling went on, like, FOREVER.

Or at least, until we were RUDELY interrupted.

"Hello, people!" MacKenzie announced as she sashayed into the room. "Here I am!"

Then she dropped her Prada bag right on the stack of pictures I was sorting for Brandon.

BRANDON AND ME, GETTING RUDELY
INTERRUPTED

I rolled my eyes at MacKenzie while Brandon looked superannoyed.

Then she gave him a big fat phony smile. "Brandon, I just had the most brilliant idea. You're going to be so thankful to me. But I need to talk to you about it ALONE!" she said in a breathy voice while batting her eyes like someone had thrown a fistful of sand in her face or something.

OMG! Watching that girl shamelessly flirt with Brandon like that was SO disgusting I actually threw up in my mouth a little.

Suddenly MacKenzie looked at me and scrunched up her nose like she smelled a funky foot odor. "Nikki, what are you doing in here? Don't you know this room is for experienced journalists only?"

"What I want to know is, WHY are YOU dressed like a tacky flight attendant?" I responded. "Are you here to write or to hand out peanuts?"

MACKENZIE AS A TACKY FLIGHT ATTENDANT

"PEANUTS FOR YOU. AND PEANUTS FOR YOU.
EVERYONE GETS SOME PEANUTS!!"

Brandon snickered but quickly covered it with a
fake cough.

Hey! SHE started the fashion critiques with her doggie-sweater comment. I just finished it.

MacKenzie let out a high-pitched laugh, like she was in on the joke. But her eyes were shooting daggers at me.

"So, what are you working on today?" she asked Brandon, peering over his shoulder. Then she picked up a photo of a puppy.

"OMG! I LOVE puppies. Are they from that place called Fuzzy Friends? I heard they are closing down. I just hope those poor creatures won't be put to sleep. That'd be AWFUL! Hey, I have a great idea! Maybe I could help out by ska—"

Brandon's jaw tightened as he gritted his teeth. "Actually, MacKenzie, Nikki and I are working on a really important project. We're kind of busy right now. So if you don't mind, um . . ." He coughed again.

MacKenzie definitely got the hint.

"Oh! Well . . . I didn't mean to interrupt anything. I just stopped by to get my, um . . ." She looked around the room frantically until she spotted something on the floor.

"My . . . PAPER CLIP! Yep, it's right here. I accidentally dropped it on the floor yesterday, and I've been looking everywhere for it! Thank goodness I found it!"

"I'm really happy for you, MacKenzie," I said sarcastically.

"Well, I guess I'll just talk to you later, Brandon. When you're not so . . ." She shot me an evil look. "BUSY. Good-bye!"

She plastered a fake smile across her face, winked

at Brandon, and sashayed out of the room. I just HATE it when MacKenzie sashays.

It was quite obvious she had come to talk to Brandon about skating for Fuzzy Friends. And then she created all of that drama over a lost paper clip. How totally JUVENILE was that?!

Chloe, Zoey, and I are planning to stop by the shelter on Saturday to talk to Betty, the owner. I just hope we get to her before MacKenzie does. I think MacKenzie is also CRAZY jealous that Brandon and I have been spending more time together lately.

But girlfriend needs to:

1. Cry a river.

2. Build a bridge, AND

3. GET OVER IT!!

☺!!

AAAAAHHHHH! That is me SCREAMING.

WHY? I HATE taking those six-hour standardized tests for math, science, and reading comprehension!

You know, the one where your normally nice and friendly teacher suddenly turns into a MAXIMUM-SECURITY PRISON GUARD and marches around the room slapping the test booklet on your desk.

← FORMERLY NICE TEACHER

SLAP!!

SLAP!!

Then, at the beginning of the test, she clicks this little stopwatch and yells . . .

"YOU MAY BEGIN . . . NOW!"

And at the end of the test, she clicks the little stopwatch again and yells . . .

"PLEASE STOP . . . NOW!"

Then she says, "Put DOWN your pencil! Do NOT turn the page. Put your HANDS above your HEAD. You have the right to remain silent. Anything you say can and will be used against you. You have the right to an attorney . . ."

OMG! It's enough to scare the snot right out of you! No wonder students perform so poorly on these tests. But the worst part is that they compare your test scores with the scores of kids in your state and across the nation. This makes YOU look really BAD because the kids from those faraway schools are never as STUPID as the kids in your OWN school!

And since stupidity is more CONTAGIOUS than chicken pox, there is no way you can beat the test scores from those other schools.

Especially when you sit next to a seventeen-year-old guy who's STILL in eighth grade and STILL eats boogers.

So, under the circumstances, WHY would you even TRY to do well on the test when you already know your score is going to be LOUSY? I'm just sayin'!

That's why I'd like to see a CONNECT-THE-DOTS standardized test. Each student fills in those little circles on his/her answer sheet, and the test score is based on how CUTE and CREATIVE his/her picture is.

This type of testing would be more FAIR and, most important, a lot EASIER ☺!

I can't wait to score in the top 1% of the nation with all those smarty-pants AND earn an academic scholarship to Harvard University.

All because of my FABULOUS masterpiece!! . . .

BUTTERFLY BLISS IN #2 PENCIL

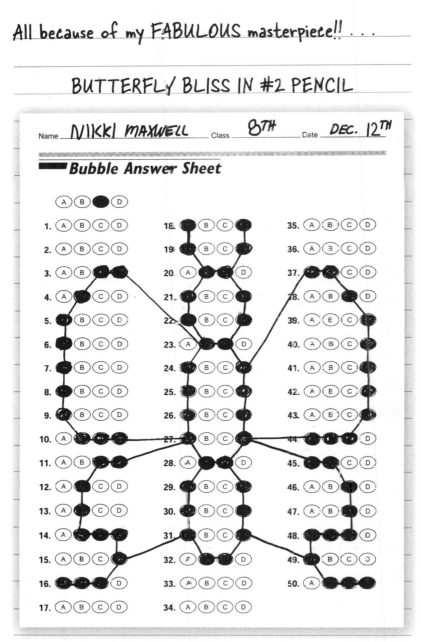

Am I not brilliant??!! ☺!!

I'm so upset right now I can barely write!

I've been in my room crying for the past two hours.

And I still don't have the slightest idea what I'm going to do about the situation.

After we dropped off Brianna at her ballet class at 5:00 p.m., my mom decided to buy some poinsettias and holiday centerpieces for our house.

She actually chose the flower shop right next to FUZZY FRIENDS!!

It was an amazing coincidence because Chloe, Zoey, and I were planning to go there tomorrow.

Mom told me she'd be in the flower shop about fifteen minutes and she'd meet me back at the car. So I rushed over to Fuzzy Friends and prayed that Betty would be in the office.

Just inside the front door I saw a stack of empty moving boxes, and my heart sank.

It looked like I was already too late!

I peeked inside a well—lit office and saw an older lady taking pictures off the walls.

"Excuse me! Are you Betty?" I asked.

"Yes, I am, dear. Come right in. This is the perfect time to adopt one of our pets, because we're going to be closing our doors real soon. Are you interested in a dog or cat?" She picked up a clipboard and gave me a big smile.

I immediately liked her.

And now I understand why Brandon likes her so much too.

"I'll need you to fill out a few forms. But the good news is that there's no charge at all!"

"Actually, I'm not here to adopt a pet. Although they're quite adorable. I was here last week as a student volunteer. And now I'm wondering if we could represent Fuzzy Friends in a school—related community service project?"

Betty motioned for me to sit down.

"Well, first of all, thank you for volunteering!" she said. "It's the wonderful and caring people like you who have allowed us to place more than two hundred animals so far this year. But unfortunately, a few days ago my husband fell off a ladder while painting the kitchen and broke his leg in two places. There's just no way we can continue to stay open."

I didn't waste any time and immediately explained the *Holiday on Ice* program and how the money we earned could be used to help keep the center open for a few months. Hopefully, until her husband fully recovered.

Betty became overwhelmed with emotion and suddenly burst into tears. . . .

I wasn't the least bit surprised to hear what she said next.

"You know what?! Now that I think about it, I got a telephone message yesterday from a young lady about *Holiday on Ice*. But I assumed she was selling tickets. I think her name was Madison. Or was it Mikaya—"

"MACKENZIE?"

"Yes! That's it. MacKenzie! How did you know?"

"Oh! Just a lucky guess."

"Well, Nikki! Tell me how I can sign up Fuzzy Friends as a *Holiday on Ice* charity! I'm really looking forward to seeing you and your friends skate."

Our meeting went even better than I could have imagined.

She gave me her business card with her home telephone number and even the hospital number so I could reach her pretty much 24-7.

"Nikki, you have no idea how much this means to me, my husband, and especially our grandson," Betty gushed. "Poor little guy! He's already been through so much, losing his parents a few years ago. And now we were going to have to uproot him and move to a new state in the middle of the year. I was dreading having to break the news to him, but thanks to you, I won't have to. He's out back exercising the dogs. All I can say is thank you, thank you!" Then she hugged me so hard, I could barely breathe.

"Thank YOU! For agreeing to be our charity and allowing us to skate for you," I said, tearing up a little myself. "We'll try to make Fuzzy Friends proud!"

As I left the shelter I noticed a tall fence that surrounded the entire property.

I heard what sounded like a pack of dogs barking excitedly and couldn't help but sneak a peek.

I saw a boy running around with what appeared to be eight dogs of assorted sizes, colors, and breeds, including the three puppies.

Even though his back was to me, I could see he had one of those soft foam rubber footballs and seemed to be having a rousing football game of guy versus dogs. . . .

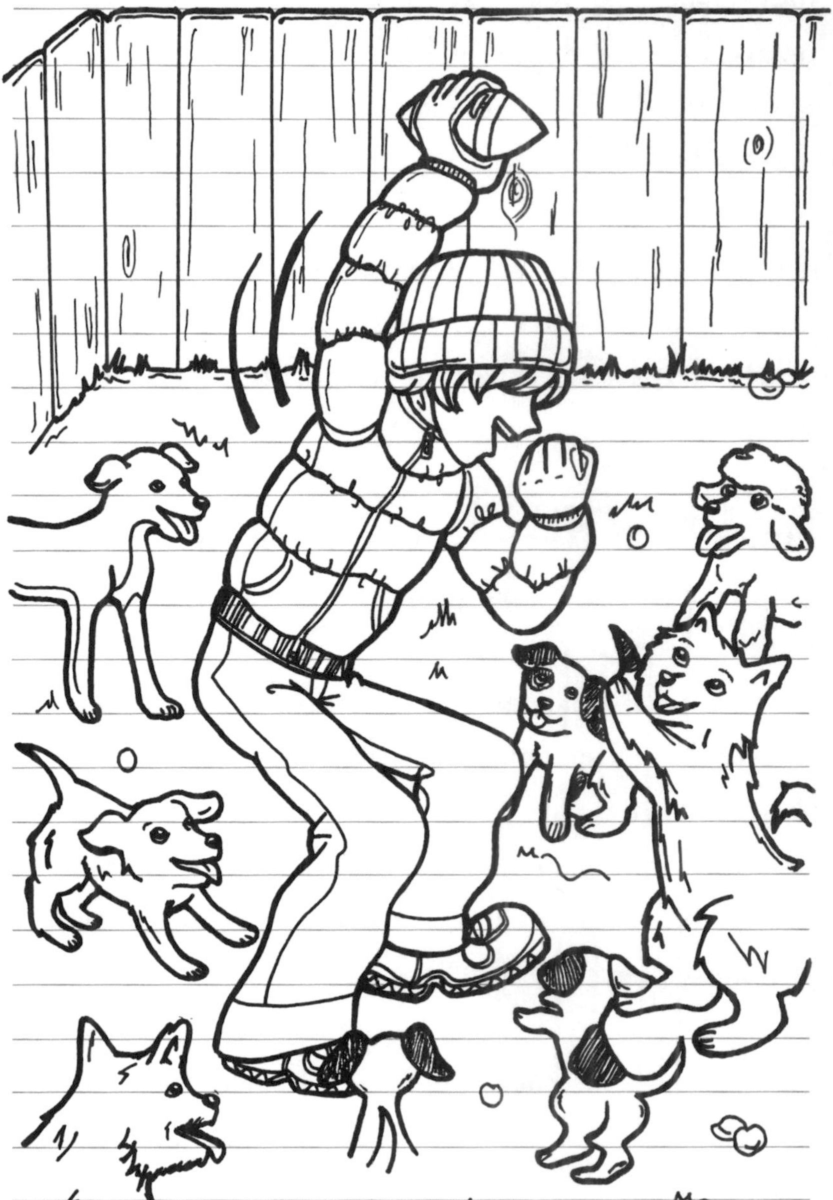

He ran with the football across the grass, dodging imaginary tackles, as the dogs happily chased after him, barking and nipping at his heels.

"And it's a TOUCHDOWN!!" he screamed. "And the CROWD GOES WILD!! HAAAAAARRR!"

That's when I noticed his voice sounded vaguely familiar.

But my brain refused to make the connection and instead decided he must just sound like someone I knew.

The boy spiked the football into the ground and broke into a funky chicken/running man/Dougie-inspired victory dance as the dogs barked and ran in frenzied circles around him.

Then he and all the dogs collapsed on the ground in sheer exhaustion.

When I finally saw his face, I froze and gasped in shock. . . .

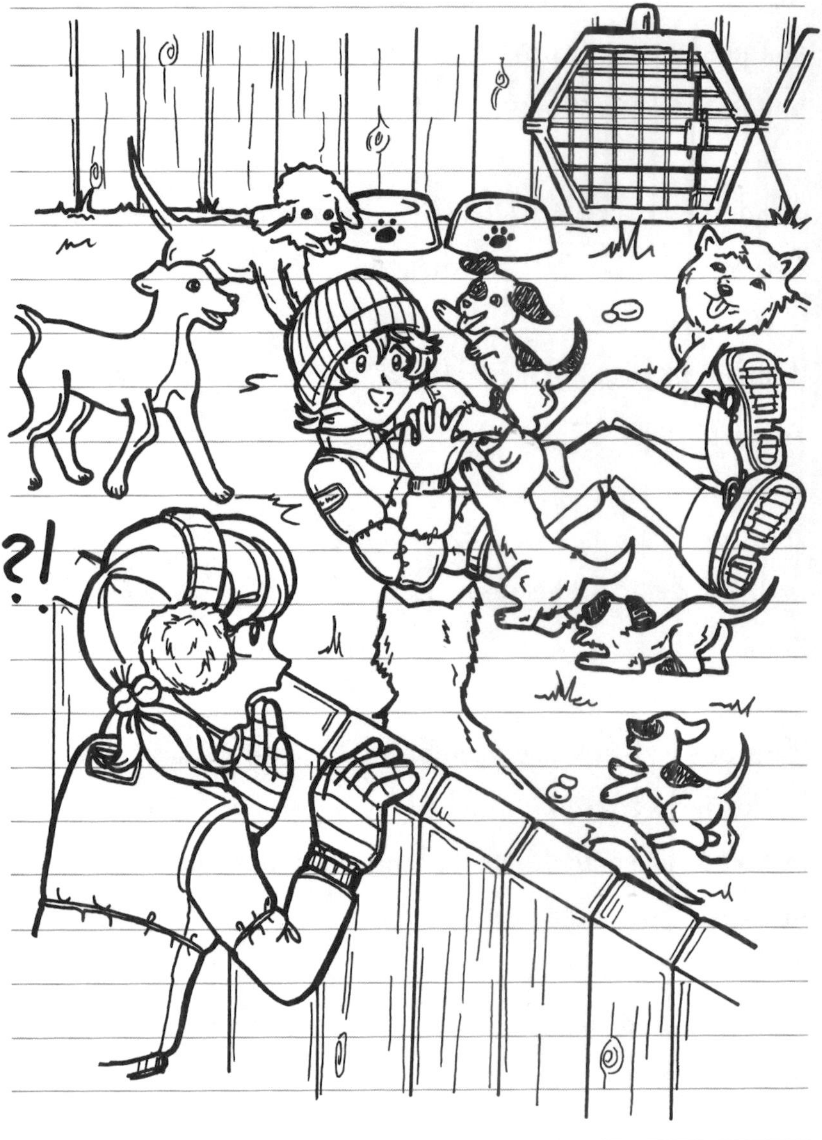
?!

IT WAS BRANDON!!

Suddenly that comment he made a couple days ago, about never forgetting me no matter what happened, took on a whole new meaning.

He KNEW that IF Fuzzy Friends closed, there was a chance he and his grandparents might be moving away during the holiday break!

NOOO! THIS CAN'T BE HAPPENING!! OMG! OMG! OMG!

Brandon and I might not EVER see each other AGAIN! ☹!!

SATURDAY, DECEMBER 14

The shock about Brandon is finally starting to wear off a little.

But I still have a million questions:

WHO is Brandon, really?

WHERE is he from?

WHAT happened to his parents?

WHEN did he start living with his grandparents?

HOW did he end up at WCD?

And what about all that stuff I overheard MacKenzie and Jessica saying about Brandon in the bathroom?! Is any of that true?

Just thinking about all this is enough to make my head spin and my heart hurt.

I can't begin to imagine what he's gone through.

But I don't dare breathe a word of this to another living soul. Not even Chloe and Zoey.

If Brandon wants anyone to know, he can tell them.

Well, at least something good happened today. I mailed off the paperwork, so now it's official!

Chloe, Zoey, and I will be skating in the *Holiday on Ice* show for the charity Fuzzy Friends!

And I plan to do everything within my power to help keep that place open.

For the animals.

For Betty and Phil.

And most important, for . . . BRANDON!

I <u>KNOW</u> I CAN DO THIS. ☺!!

ARRRGH!!

I'm so ticked off at Brianna and Miss Penelope right now, I could just . . . SCREAM!!

But since this whole thing was Mom's STUPID idea, it's technically all HER fault!

You'd think that after giving birth to two children, she would be a more responsible parent!

Why in the world would she ask ME to take over the family tradition of baking holiday cookies for friends and neighbors?!

I should have suspected that something was up when Mom started acting really weird at dinner.

After setting the table, she just stood there, like a mannequin or something, holding on to my chair and staring at me with this strange look on her face.

But since I was pretty much starving, I just ignored her and continued to stuff my face.

Suddenly Mom's eyes glazed over and she stopped blinking. This could mean only one thing.

She'd somehow suffered a head injury while fixing the meat loaf and needed emergency medical care. Or maybe NOT.

"Mom! Are you okay?!" I said through a mouthful of food.

"Oh!" She suddenly snapped out of her daze as a big sappy grin spread across her face. "I was just thinking about how wonderful it would be to pass my cookie tradition on to YOU, so that one day you can share it with YOUR daughter."

"HUH?!" I gasped, almost choking on my mashed potatoes.

WHY were we talking about BABIES?!

Brandon and I HADN'T even held hands yet!

I was happy Mom had such pleasant memories of

baking cookies with me when I was a little kid. . . .

MOM AND ME (AT AGE FIVE),
BAKING HOLIDAY COOKIES

Sorry! But I was so NOT looking forward to baking cookies with my OWN daughter.

Mainly because I had this fear she would be a little TERROR as punishment for all the HEADACHES I had caused my mom. . . .

ME AND MY DAUGHTER (AT AGE FIVE),
BAKING HOLIDAY COOKIES

That's when Mom placed her hands on my shoulders and looked into my eyes.

"Nikki, will you make the Christmas cookies this year?! It would mean so very much to me."

My gut reaction was to scream, "Mom, stop it! You're SCARING me!"

But instead I just shrugged, swallowed a hunk of meat loaf, and muttered, "Um . . . okay."

I mean, how hard could baking cookies be? Moms do it all the time. Right?!

After dinner was over, Mom handed me the cookie recipe so I could get started. Then she headed for the mall to finish up her Christmas shopping.

The thing that bothered me most was that Mom had very conveniently left out an important detail. I had to bake cookies with BRIANNA. ☹!!

I tried to cook a gourmet dinner with Brianna back in September, and it was a total disaster.

And I was STILL haunted by the horrible memory of making homemade ice cream at Thanksgiving and both Brianna and Dad getting their tongues stuck on the metal ice cream thingy!

Brianna came skipping into the kitchen.

"Hi, Nikki! Guess what? Me and Miss Penelope are here to help you bake cookies!"

I was like, JUST GREAT ☹!!

I knew I had to keep Brianna really busy so she wouldn't get in my way or do something predictably dangerous.

Like stuff Miss Penelope in the microwave on the popcorn setting to see if she would magically turn into a bucket of popcorn.

So to distract Brianna, I asked her to go find me two cookie sheets.

Things got off to a great start. I had measured all the ingredients and was about to start mixing.

That's when Brianna started making so much noise, it sounded like a construction work site.

CLANK! BANG! KLUNK! CLANK!

"Brianna, I can barely hear myself think! Stop making all that noise before you make my head explode!" I yelled.

Her eyes lit up. "Really? This noise will make your head explode? COOL!"

CLANK! BANG! KLUNK!

"Brianna! Knock it off! Or I'm calling Mom . . . !" I threatened.

"Look at me!" she said, doing the robot around the kitchen. "I'm the Tin Man from *The Wizard of Oz!*"

BRIANNA, AS THE TIN MAN

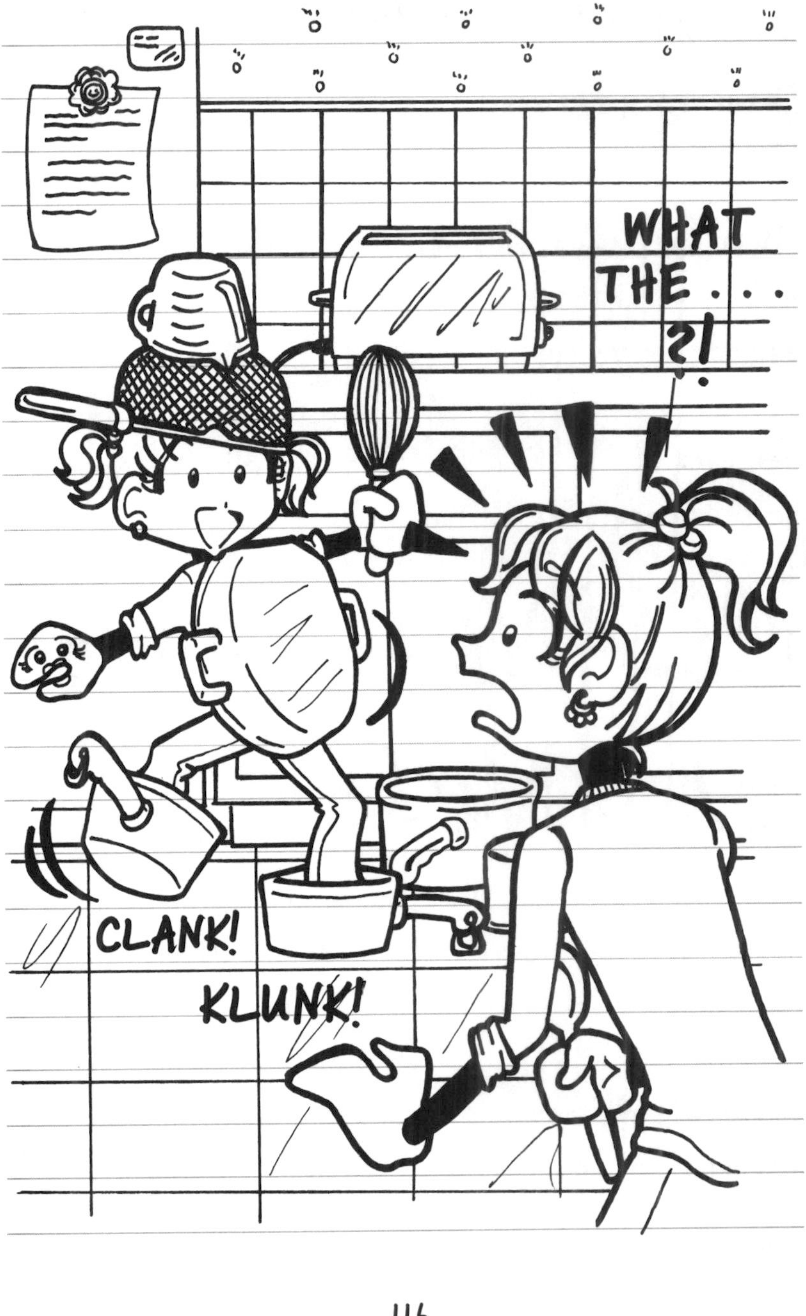
WHAT THE . . . ?!
CLANK!
KLUNK!

"Sorry, Brianna! You're NOT the Tin Man," I muttered. "You need a BRAIN! THAT would make you the SCARECROW!"

"Nikki! I do got a BRAIN!" she huffed. "SEE?" She opened her mouth really wide and pointed.

I pulled out a chair from the kitchen table and set it in front of her.

"Just sit here and don't move, like a good little Tin Man. Just pretend you're rusting or something. Okay?"

I mixed the cookie ingredients together, rolled out the dough, and made little Christmas trees with Mom's cookie cutters.

Then I placed the cookies in the oven. When I turned around, Brianna was licking the spoon.

"Brianna, don't lick the spoon! I need to use it to make this last batch of cookies."

"It's Miss Penelope's fault, not mine. She's tasting the cookie dough to make sure it's not nasty. She says you're really good at drawing, but your cooking STINKS!"

I could NOT believe Miss Penelope was talking trash about me like that. Especially since she wasn't even a real . . . um . . . HUMAN.

I thought about grabbing the rolling pin and giving Miss Penelope something really nasty to "taste."

But instead I decided to chillax by watching TV in the family room while my cookies baked for thirteen minutes.

It hadn't been more than five minutes when I thought I smelled something burning.

I rushed back into the kitchen, and Brianna was standing near the stove with this really guilty look on her face.

The oven temperature had been changed from 350 degrees to BROIL! This is what happened. . . .

I told Miss Penelope NOT to turn the oven on high. But she wanted the cookies to get done fast 'cause she's really HUNGRY!

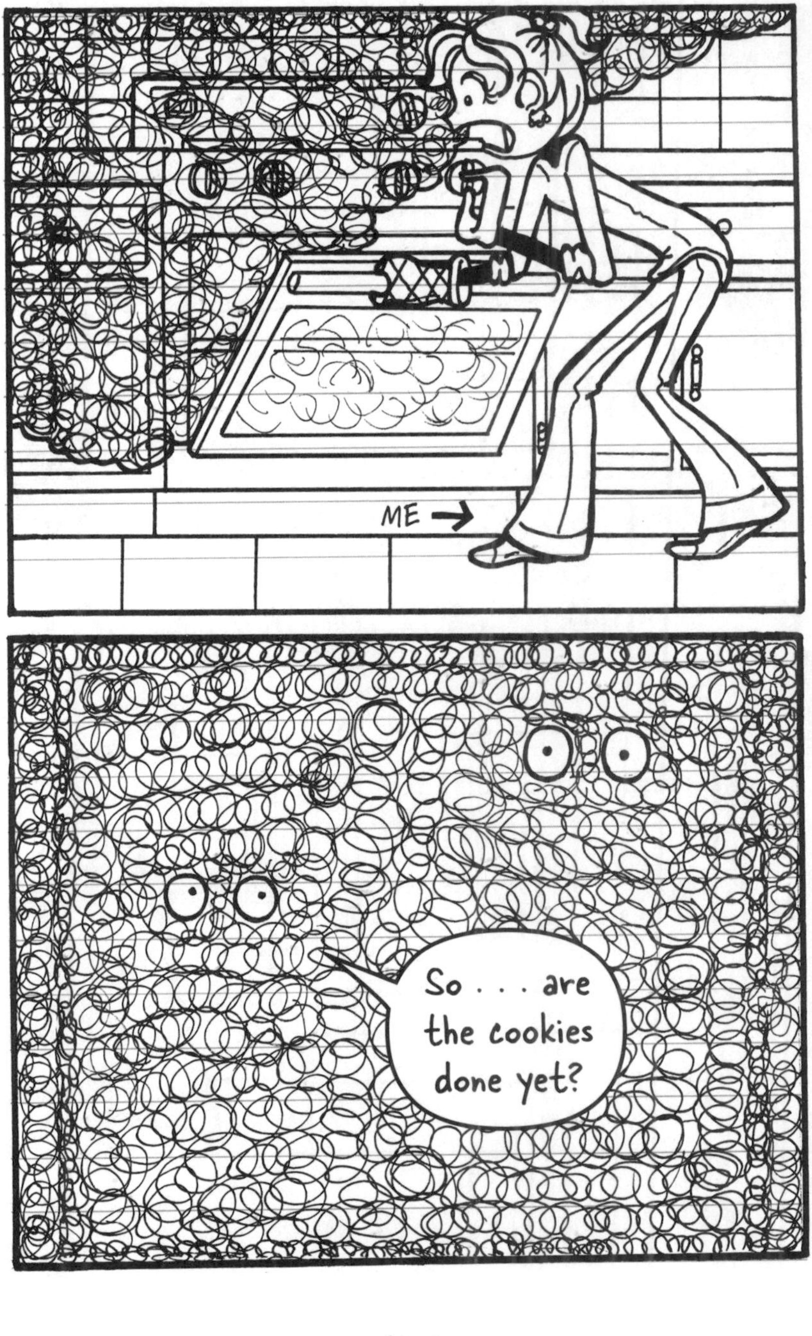
ME
So . . . are the cookies done yet?

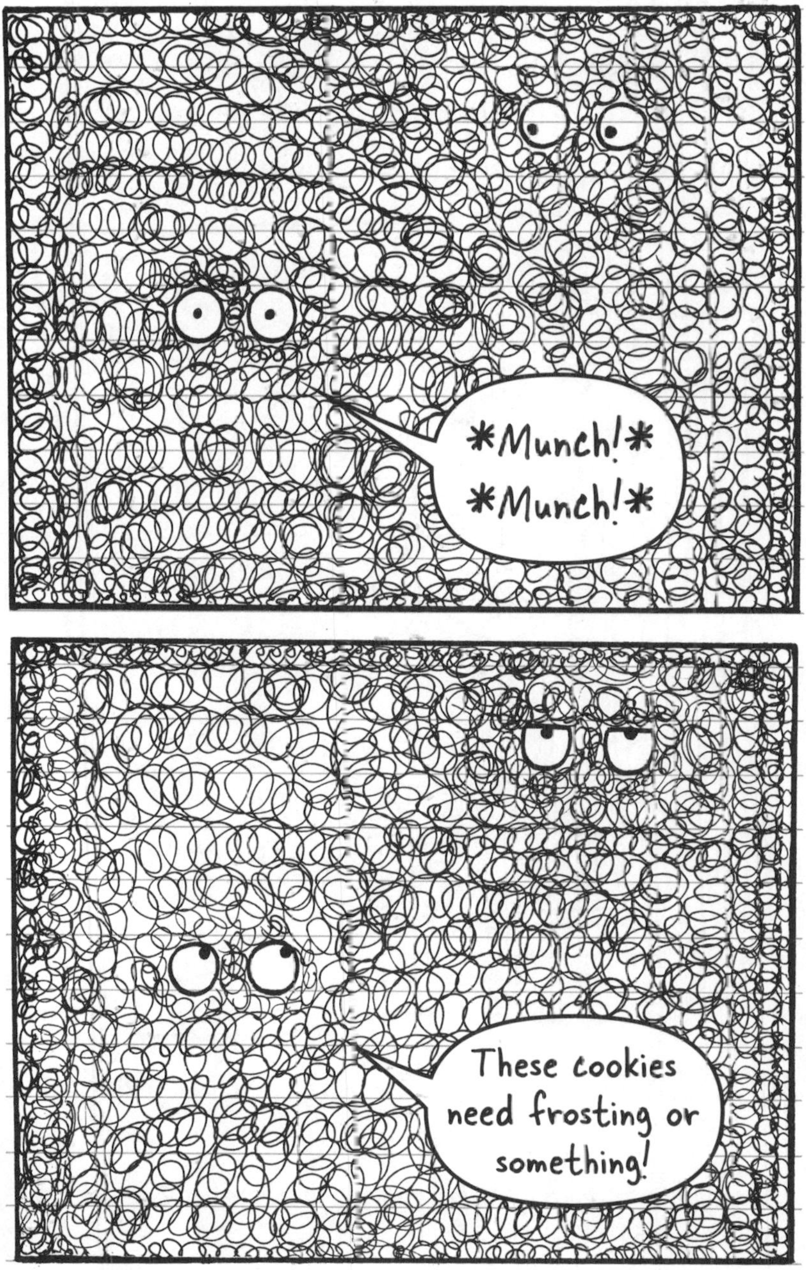
Munch! *Munch!*
These cookies need frosting or something!

I opened the windows to clear out all the smoke and hoped the fire department wouldn't show up. OMG! I'll just DIE if my face ends up plastered on the front page of the city newspaper!

ME, PLASTERED ACROSS THE FRONT PAGE

This little baking project was a complete and utter DISASTER!

Now I have to call Mom and break the news that she needs to stop by the grocery store on her way home from the mall.

Because this year, thanks to Brianna and Miss Penelope, all our friends and family members will be receiving holiday cookies baked in a hollow tree by those little Keebler Elves! I'm just sayin' . . . ☹!!

I can't believe that we actually start ice-skating in gym class tomorrow. Soon I'll be gliding across the ice and doing double-axel jumps like the pros.

I plan to go to bed an hour early tonight so I'll be alert and well rested.

It's going to be weird hanging around Brandon now that I know his situation. I'm still really worried about him.

But I think I'm starting to like him even MORE! ☺!!

Right now I'm SO frustrated I could just . . .

SCREAM ☹!!

Today was my first day of ice-skating at the high school arena during gym class, and it was a complete DISASTER!

Just standing up on the ice was, like, ten times harder than I thought it was going to be.

WHY, WHY, WHY did I ever agree to do this stupid Holiday on Ice show?!

I must have been temporarily INSANE.

And it didn't help matters that MacKenzie was FUMING over the fact that Chloe, Zoey, and I were skating for Fuzzy Friends, and not HER.

As usual, that girl went out of her way to make my life MISERABLE. . . .

I can't believe MacKenzie actually said that right to my face like that.

The entire class heard it too. It seemed like everyone was snickering about me behind my back.

OMG! I was beyond HUMILIATED!

We were SUPPOSED to be practicing our *Holiday on Ice* skating routine during gym class.

But NOOOO! I didn't practice at all. WHY?!!

BECAUSE I'M SO HORRIBLY CRUDDY AT ICE-SKATING, I COULDN'T EVEN STAND UP! THAT'S WHY!!

Chloe and Zoey even held both my hands like I was a clumsy little toddler taking my first steps. But I STILL fell down!

The ONLY thing I could do really well was a move that required superwobbly legs.

127

Well, I'm really sorry to disappoint those snobby CCPs! But any dance I was doing was PURELY accidental.

Chloe and Zoey told me to chillax and be patient because it might take three or four weeks of practice before I could even skate around the rink by myself.

But our ice show is in only TWO WEEKS!! Girlfriends, do the MATH!!

Zoey suggested that I read her book *Figure Skating for Dummies*.

And Chloe offered to loan me her novel *The Ice Princess*.

But personally, I don't think books are going to help me much.

The only TWO things I really NEED right now are:

One of those walker thingies that really old people

use, because six legs on the ice are better than just two . . .

And a really soft pillow because I now have a dozen bruises from falling on my behind, and I'm NOT going to be able to sit down for a week. . . .

Unfortunately, we'll be practicing our ice-skating routine in gym class for the rest of the week.

And then on December 26, 27, and 30, we have three special practice sessions for the December 31 show.

I don't mean to be all doom-'n'-gloom, but this ice-skating stuff is turning into a total NIGHTMARE!

AAAAAAHHHHHH!!!!

That was me screaming in frustration. AGAIN!

But I have to remain calm and stay focused.

I can't afford to fail. Because if I do, Brandon will be forced to move, and he's had enough trauma in his life.

OMG! WHAT have I gotten myself into??!

☹!!

I'm sitting in my bedroom trying not to have a
TOTAL MELTDOWN.

I just HATE it when I do things at the very last
minute.

My *Moby-Dick* assignment is due in less than
fourteen hours and I'm just now starting it.

By "it" I don't mean the book REPORT.

I'm just starting to READ the stupid BOOK ☹!!

My biggest fear is that the book might aggravate
a very serious medical problem.

You see, I'm superALLERGIC to . . . BORING!

There's a possibility that while I'm reading
Moby-Dick, I could have a SEVERE allergic reaction
due to extreme BOREDOM and go into anaphylactic
shock.

I could, like, actually . . . *DIE!!*

MY PAINFUL AND SENSELESS DEATH FROM SEVERE BOREDOM DUE TO READING MOBY-DICK

Then my teacher would give me a big fat INCOMPLETE for my grade because I didn't finish the assignment!

OMG! What if she made me attend SUMMER

SCHOOL to make up for the incomplete?! How CRUDDY would THAT be?!

Thank goodness I'd already be DEAD due to my allergic reaction to boredom ☺!!

Anyway, I had no idea how I was going to read the entire 672-page book AND write a report. But I was DETERMINED to do it.

So I pulled out my *Moby-Dick* book and started reading as fast as my little eyeballs could go.

The good news was that if I read six pages a minute, I could finish the book in less than two hours ☺!!

I was pleasantly surprised when I didn't immediately doze off or have any major medical complications from my boredom allergy.

But after what seemed like forever, I was so mentally exhausted, the words were just a blur on the page. That's when I decided to stop and take a short fifteen-minute break from my intensive reading.

Especially since, according to my clock, I'd been reading for an entire seven minutes AND had blazed my way through three whole pages.

After quickly recalculating my numbers, I made a very shocking and grim discovery.

At the rate I was currently working, it was going to take me FOREVER to read the book, assuming I DIDN'T stop to rest, eat, get a drink of water, sleep, or go to the bathroom.

I was so NOT happy about this situation.

That's when I suddenly got this overwhelming urge to rip the pages out of that book one by one and flush them down the TOILET while hopping on one foot.

DON'T ASK! I was suffering from mental exhaustion.

How BAD did I NOT want to read *Moby-Dick*?

I actually made a list. . . .

5 THINGS I'D RATHER DO THAN READ *MOBY-DICK*

1. Pluck out my eye with a dirty spatula
2. Clean every toilet in the house with a toothbrush
3. Brush my teeth with the toothbrush I used to clean every toilet in the house
4. Visit our neighbor lady, Mrs. Wallabanger, for a detailed update on her bunion surgery
5. Hang out with Brianna

HANG OUT WITH BRIANNA?!

I could NOT believe I actually wrote those words.

Especially after she totally grossed me out at dinner tonight.

HOW?

By opening her mouth to show me her partially chewed broccoli tuna casserole.

While Hawaiian Punch dribbled out of her nose.

OMG! It was all so NASTY I couldn't even finish my meal!

It's making me queasy again just thinking about it.

Finally, I'd had enough. I slammed my *Moby-Dick* book shut and threw it across the room in utter frustration.

Then I walked down the hall and stuck my head inside Brianna's room.

"Hey, Brianna! What's up?"

She was sprawled on the floor playing dolls.

"The Wicked Witch has thrown Princess Sugar Plum into the ocean, and Baby Unicorn is trying to rescue her. But since he can't swim, the Magic Baby Dolphin has to help," Brianna explained.

"Sounds fun!" I said.

"Do you wanna play too?" Brianna asked excitedly.

"Sure!" I said, and flopped down on the floor next to her.

Okay, what was more important?

Spending quality time with my wonderful little sister?

Or reading *Moby-Dick*?

Mom would have been proud!

Brianna picked up her Magic Baby Dolphin and changed her voice to a high squeak. "Hurry, Baby

Unicorn! Jump into My Designer Dream Boat and we'll go rescue Princess Sugar Plum."

I placed Baby Unicorn on the boat and did my best impression of Alvin from *Alvin and the Chipmunks.* "Okay, let's go! Thank you, Magic Baby Dolphin, for helping me! How will I ever repay you?"

"You can come to my birthday party and bring lots of candy! I'm going to have a pizza party at Queasy Cheesy. With chocolate cake, too," Brianna said happily.

"Oooh! Goody gumdrops! I just LOVE Queasy Cheesy! And chocolate cake," ~~I said~~ Baby Unicorn said.

"Just keep an eye out for sharks!" Magic Baby Dolphin added. "They have very pointy teeth, you know!"

"AAAHHH! SHARKS! Get me outta here!!" Baby Unicorn screamed as she ran and hid.

"Wait! Come back, Baby Unicorn! Who's going to

save Princess Sugar Plum?!" Magic Baby Dolphin cried.

"I dunno! Call 911! Sharks have very pointy teeth. And I'm allergic to very pointy teeth!" Baby Unicorn screamed hysterically.

Brianna giggled. "Nikki! This is just like the Princess Sugar Plum MOVIE! Only, more FUN!"

That's when a little lightbulb popped on in my brain. BOAT?! FISH?! POINTY TEETH?! MOVIE?!

"Brianna! I have an idea! Let's shoot a real movie! You go run water in the bathtub, and I'll get Dad's video camera. This is going to be a blast!"

Brianna squealed with excitement. "YAY! I'm gonna go put on my Princess Sugar Plum swimsuit."

I ran back to my room and read over my *Moby-Dick* assignment sheet.

It said, "Please focus on two central themes—the allegorical significance of the whale, Moby Dick, and the deceptiveness of fate. Your report can be written or presented in any other suitable format. BE CREATIVE!"

This was GREAT news! I quickly skimmed the last few pages of *Moby-Dick*.

I felt kind of sorry for that Captain Ahab guy. In the end he was so wrapped up in his quest for revenge that he went completely overboard in his final attempt to kill that whale. No pun intended!

I quickly gathered some props. Then I auditioned my actors and cast the parts.

Of course Brianna wanted to be the STAR of the movie. And since none of those teen actors from the Disney and Nickelodeon channels were available on such short notice, I finally gave in and let her do it.

MOBY-DICK—CAST OF CHARACTERS

ISHMAEL, narrator and member of *Pequod* whaling ship crew

(Played by Kent fashion doll)

CAPTAIN AHAB, crazy captain of the *Pequod.* Totally obsessed with killing the whale, Moby Dick, after it bit off his leg.

(Played by Wicked Witch of the West doll)

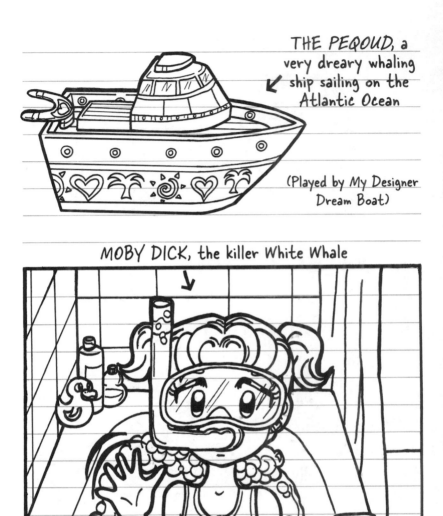

THE *PEQOUD*, a very dreary whaling ship sailing on the Atlantic Ocean

(Played by My Designer Dream Boat)

MOBY DICK, the killer White Whale

(Played by Brianna Maxwell)

Shooting our movie was pretty challenging. To create the stormy ocean, I decided to use a fan.

OKAY! LIGHTS, CAMERA, ACTION!

ROAR!!

We finished filming in about an hour. I think my movie turned out pretty good. Especially considering the fact that I had a cast of inexperienced actors and no budget, and it wasn't shot on location.

I just hope I get a decent grade.

But most important, I learned a very crucial lesson about the dangers of procrastination. . . .

NEVER, EVER wait until the last minute to do a major homework assignment!

UNLESS, of course, your little sister can do a really good killer whale impersonation! ROAR!!

I'm thinking about entering my video in one of those prestigious Hollywood film festivals.

Who knows?! Maybe one day *Moby Dick Battles Princess Sugar Plum on My Designer Dream Boat* will be playing at a theater near you.

☺!!

OMG ☹!!

I have never been so HUMILIATED in my entire life!

Today in gym our teacher announced that we were going to spend the entire hour watching a very special group of skaters perform.

She said they were talented, hardworking, and deserved our utmost respect and admiration.

Next she explained that she would be scoring the skaters while the class watched.

I was so happy and relieved to hear this news that I actually did a Snoopy "happy dance" inside my head.

I'm just really bad at ice-skating. And instead of improving, I swear it seems like I'm getting WORSE.

I was looking forward to seeing those supertalented

high school kids skate. Maybe I could even learn a thing or two.

Then things got REALLY weird.

Our teacher asked MacKenzie, Chloe, Zoey, and me to stand.

Then she announced that each one of us was going to individually perform the skating routine that we were working on for the *Holiday on Ice* show.

Of course MacKenzie, Chloe, and Zoey were more than happy to show off their skills on the ice.

ME? I almost PEED my pants! Every cell in my body wanted to run out of there SCREAMING. But instead, I just shrugged and said, "Um . . . okay."

Even though MacKenzie still hadn't found a charity sponsor, her routine was sheer perfection.

On ice, she was like a graceful fairy snow princess or something. . . .

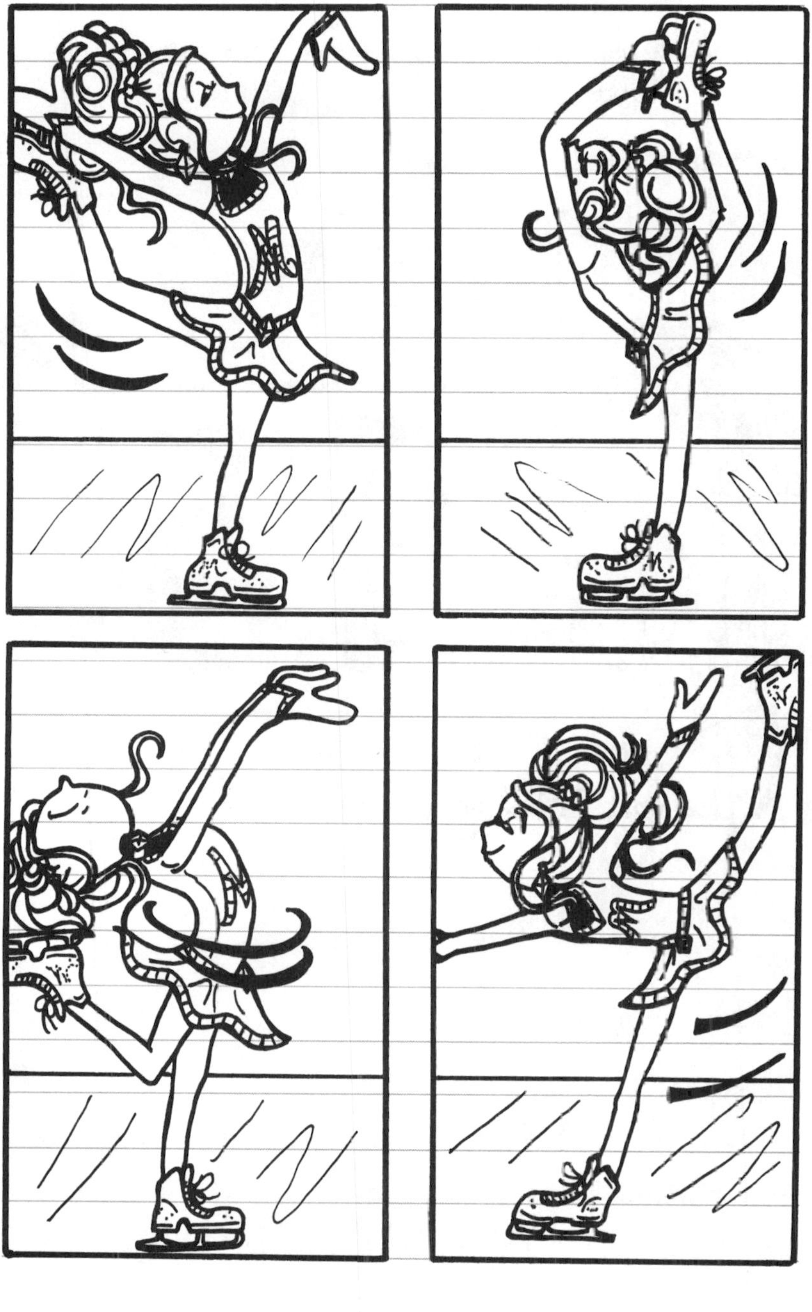

When MacKenzie finished her routine, she got a standing ovation from the class. And our gym teacher gave her a fantastic score of 9.5! I was practically green with envy.

I was up next. As I stepped onto the ice I gave myself a little pep talk. I CAN DO THIS! I CAN DO THIS! I CAN DO THIS! I CAN DO THIS!

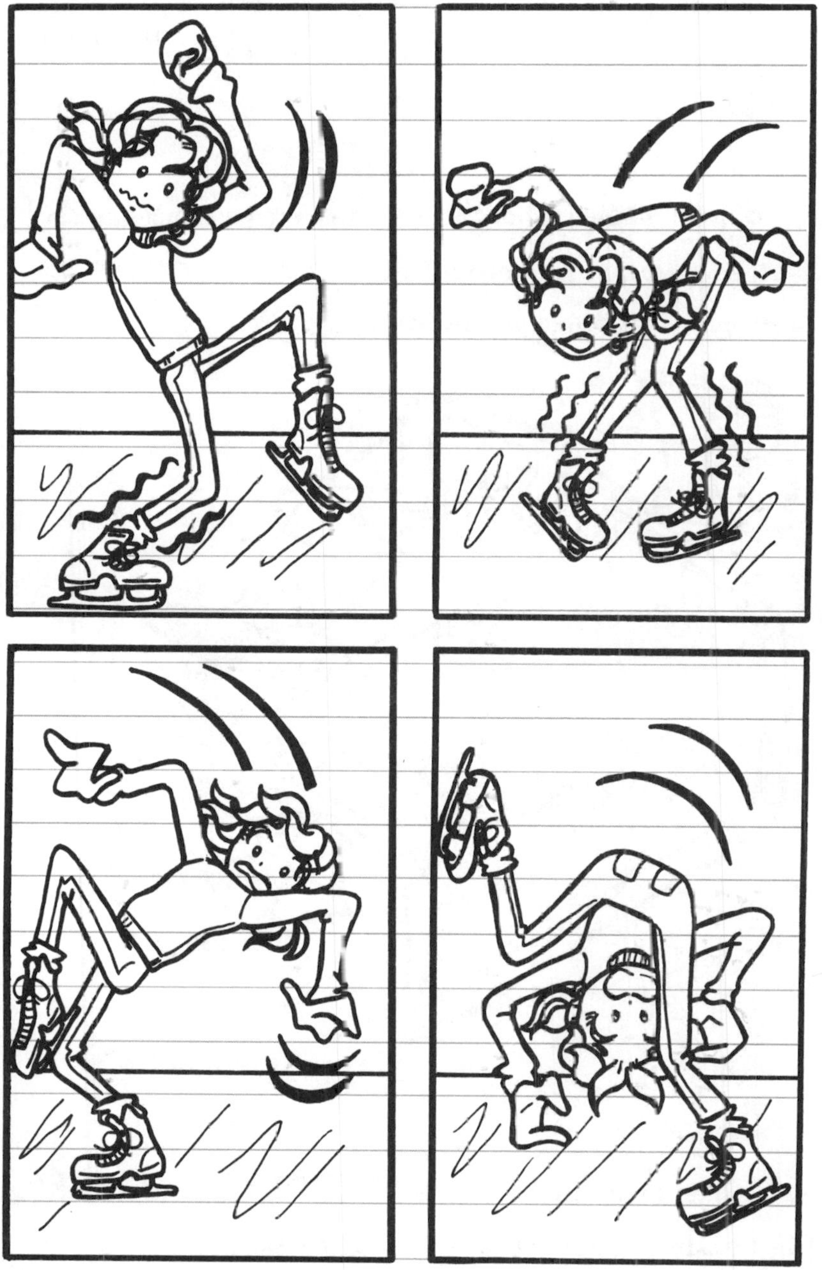

I ended my routine by tripping over my feet and sliding across the ice on my stomach like a HUMAN PUCK.

And just when I thought my skating routine couldn't get any worse, I slammed into a hockey net and it fell over, trapping me inside . . .

. . . like some kind of giant LOBSTER CREATURE in lip gloss, hoop earrings, and ice skates.

Of course all of the jocks jumped up and yelled, "GOAL!!" and gave each other high fives.

It seemed like the entire class was pointing and laughing at me. I wanted to cry really, really bad! I didn't know which hurt more, my gut or my ego.

Then, to add insult to injury, I saw my score. . . .

I could NOT believe my gym teacher had actually given me a NEGATIVE FOUR!

Hey, I'm NOT a professional judge or anything. But any IDIOT knows there are no NEGATIVE numbers in figure skating!

I was SO mad! I actually told off my teacher right in front of the entire class.

"Listen, sister! Let me see YOU get YOUR DUSTY BUTT out there on the ice and NOT BREAK A HIP or something!!"

But I just said that inside my head, so no one else heard it but me.

Chloe and Zoey rushed over to help me up and asked if I was okay.

I told them I was just fine, thank you! Then I went straight to the girls' locker room and started writing in my diary.

I'm sure Chloe and Zoey will each do really well on their routines.

Then they'll get a standing ovation from our class and a superhigh score from our teacher, just like MacKenzie!

That's because all three of them are really talented skaters.

Unlike ME!!

But I'm not jealous of them or anything.

I mean, how JUVENILE would THAT be?!!

SORRY! But I CAN'T DO THIS ANYMORE!!

I QUIT!!
☹!!

I felt really horrible giving up when so much was at stake for Brandon and his family.

But the show was only eleven days away. There was just no way I was going to be able to improve enough to NOT make a complete FOOL out of myself.

The director of the ice show is Victoria Steel, a famous Olympic gold medalist figure skater.

I heard from Chloe that she's superstrict. She yells at skaters when they fall, even though it's just a charity event. And last year she actually cut a skater from a show because she said the girl was an embarrassment!

If I stayed on the team for Fuzzy Friends, there was a risk we could get cut from the show and lose the $3,000 needed to keep the shelter open.

I couldn't take that chance.

As of yesterday, MacKenzie STILL needed a charity. So the mature and responsible thing to do was to ask BEG her to take my place and skate for Fuzzy Friends.

I really didn't have a choice in the matter.

This was the ONLY way I could help Brandon.

And YES! I felt AWFUL!

My biggest fear was that he was going to think I was an immature, undisciplined, untalented, ungraceful, self-centered BRAT!

I planned to explain everything to him tomorrow and then break the news to Chloe and Zoey.

But Brandon showed up today while I was working in the library.

Chloe and Zoey had just left to pick up several boxes of new library books from the office, and I was the only person at the front desk.

ME, NOT NOTICING BRANDON STANDING
THERE WATCHING ME WRITE IN MY DIARY

"Hey, Nikki!"

"OMG! Brandon? Hi! I didn't see you standing there!"

"So, how's the skating coming?"

"Actually, I wanted to talk to you about that. There's something I need to tell you. And I was hoping you could give Betty the message."

"Oh, really!" Brandon said, smiling. "That's funny, because I have a message from HER to YOU."

"You do? Well, you can go first," I said.

"I'm not in a big hurry. You can go first."

"No! YOU!"

I looked at him and he looked at me.

"OKAY! I'll go!" we both said at the same time.

Then we laughed.

"I give up, Maxwell. You win! I'll go first . . . ," Brandon chuckled.

Then he reached down and grabbed a bag.

"Betty asked me to give this to you. She said she wouldn't be able to keep the shelter open without your help, and it's just a small token of her appreciation."

Brandon brushed his bangs out of his eyes and gave me a big smile.

I just stared at the bag and then Brandon and then the bag and then Brandon again.

"Well?" Brandon said, still holding it out to me. "Why don't you open it? I'm supposed to make sure you like it."

As I accepted the bag from him, a big dopey smile spread across my face and I blushed profusely.

Although I was smiling on the outside, I was a complete emotional wreck on the inside.

How was I supposed to tell Brandon I was quitting the ice show when Betty had just sent me what appeared to be a thank-you gift?

Inside the bag was a small, thin gift-wrapped box. The wrapping paper had pictures of the cutest puppies wearing red bows. Just like our Great Puppy Escape photos.

But then I took a closer look. It WAS our photos! Brandon had printed them up as gift wrap.

"AWWWWW!! How cute!" I gushed.

I tore open the wrapping paper and inside was a DVD of the Disney movie *Lady and the Tramp.*

"OMG, Brandon! This was my favorite when I was a little kid! It's PERFECT!"

Brandon smiled. "I was hoping you'd like it!"

"I DO! And Brianna's going to love it too!"

Brandon crossed his arms, leaned against the desk, and stared right at me.

"So . . . what was it you wanted to tell ME?" he asked.

JUST GREAT ☹!! Right then I felt like a total JERK!

"Well, I—I just was . . . um . . . ," I stammered.

WHO would quit on a poor lady struggling with an orphaned grandson, a sick husband, and eighteen homeless animals AFTER she'd just sent a wonderful thank-you present?

Only a coldhearted SNAKE, that's who!

"Actually, it's kind of about MacKenzie."

I hesitated, staring nervously at the floor.

"She's an excellent skater, and I was thinking she—"

"Listen, Nikki. Don't worry about MacKenzie! She's been hanging around trying to get Betty to change her mind. But Betty is sticking with you, Chloe, and Zoey. Besides, in bio today I overheard MacKenzie telling Jessica she was going to be skating for a fashion school or something."

I was shocked to hear that MacKenzie had finally found a sponsor.

"A fashion school? Are you kidding?" I exclaimed. "Wait, don't tell me . . ."

I put my hand on my hip and did my best MacKenzie impression.

"Hon! Like, my very fabulous charity is from the Westchester Institute of Fashion and Cosmetology. Which, by the way, is owned by my aunt Clarissa!"

Brandon looked amused. "Yeah, actually, I think that's EXACTLY what she said. It's owned by her aunt . . . Clarissa?"

"Yeah, I bet MacKenzie convinced her aunt to start a new charity to make our city more beautiful. She stands on street corners handing out designer clothing to the fashionably challenged!" I joked.

That girl is so INCREDIBLY vain. . . .

164

MACKENZIE, MAKING OUR CITY MORE BEAUTIFUL!

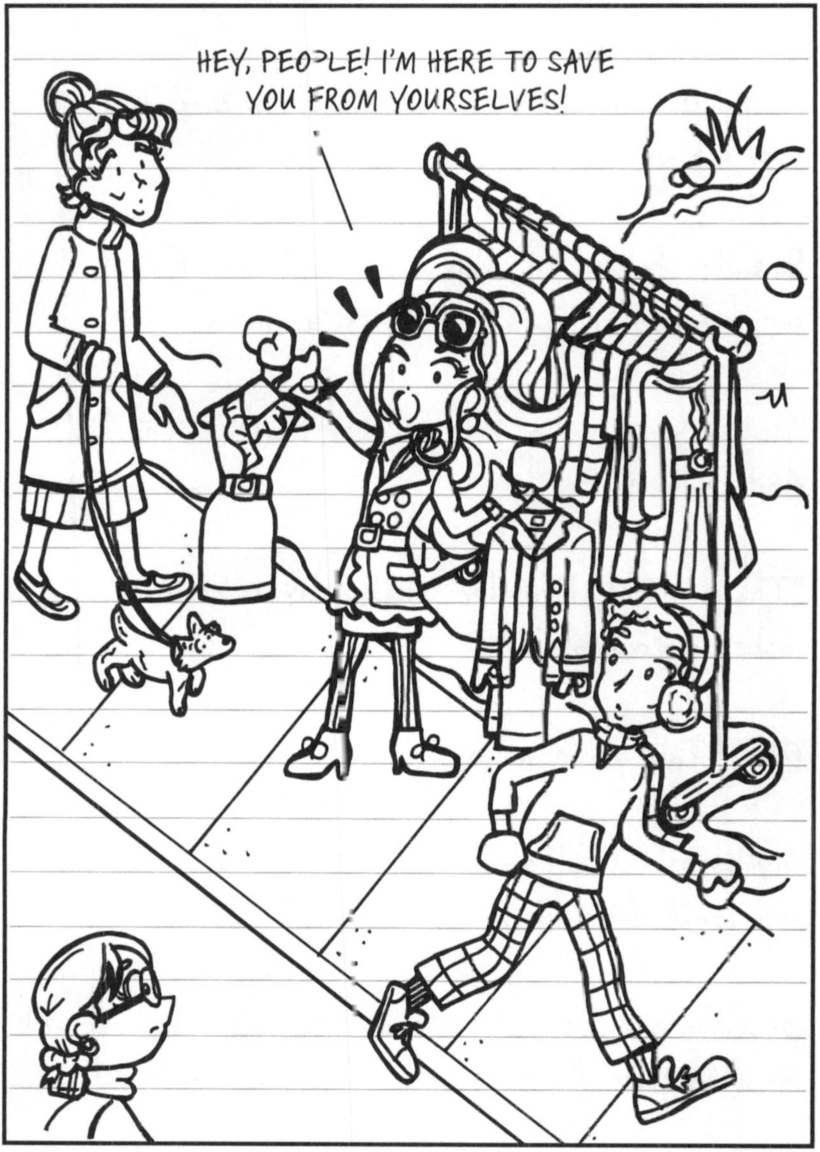
HEY, PEOPLE! I'M HERE TO SAVE YOU FROM YOURSELVES!

Thanks to her aunt Clarissa, MacKenzie was now completely OUT of the picture. Which meant ME and my very bruised behind were back IN.

I needed to go to my Emergency Plan B. Only I didn't have one.

Brandon folded his arms. "So, what is it I'm supposed to tell Betty?" he asked again.

"Actually, Brandon, just tell her I LOVE the DVD. And thanks!"

"Thank YOU!" Brandon said softly as his eyes locked onto mine.

OMG! Talk about major RCS.

My knees felt all weak and wobbly, and I wasn't even on the ice.

Brandon glanced at his watch. "Uh-oh! I better get back to class. I'm here on a . . . bathroom pass."

He gave me another one of his crooked smiles and I tried not to swoon. Very much.

After Brandon left, I collapsed into my chair.

This was BAD!

Very, very BAD!!

But when I picked up my new *Lady and the Tramp* DVD, for some reason I started to feel better.

Probably because my very favorite scene was on the cover. You know the one.

The famous SPAGHETTI KISS!

That's when I started to wonder if Brandon likes spaghetti.

What if on our very first date we went to a quaint little Italian restaurant and shared a plate of spaghetti? We'd get . . .

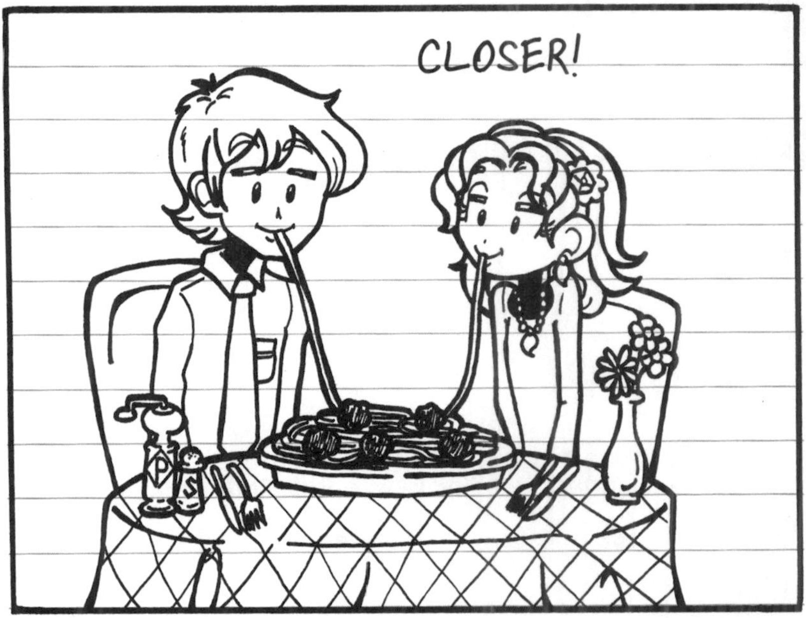
CLOSER!

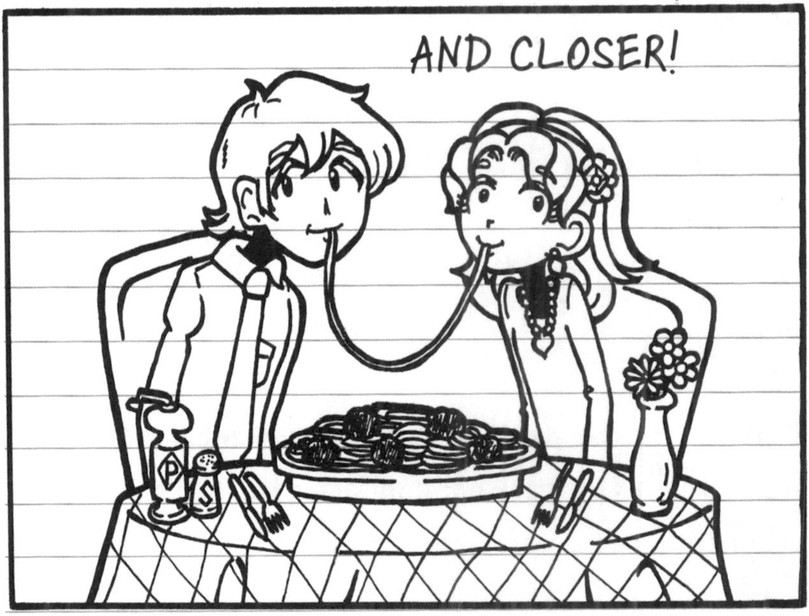
AND CLOSER!

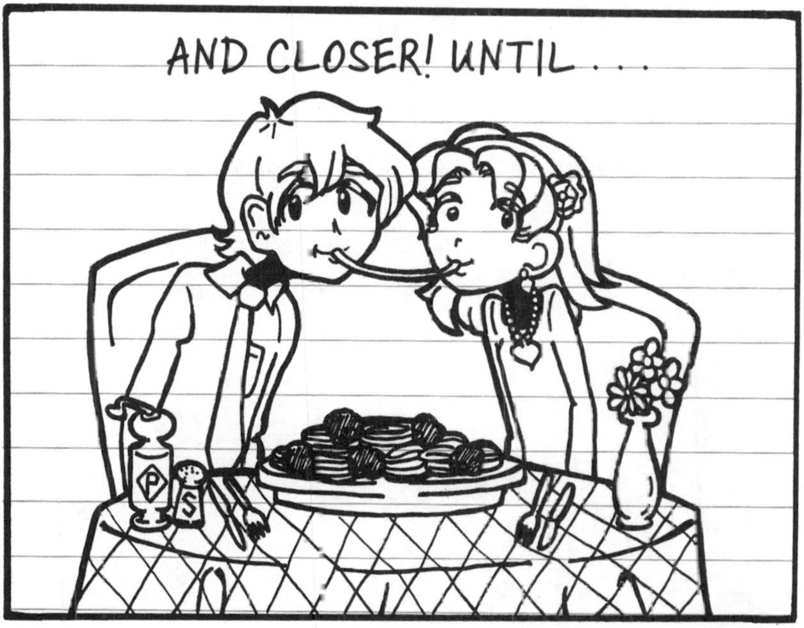
AND CLOSER! UNTIL . . .

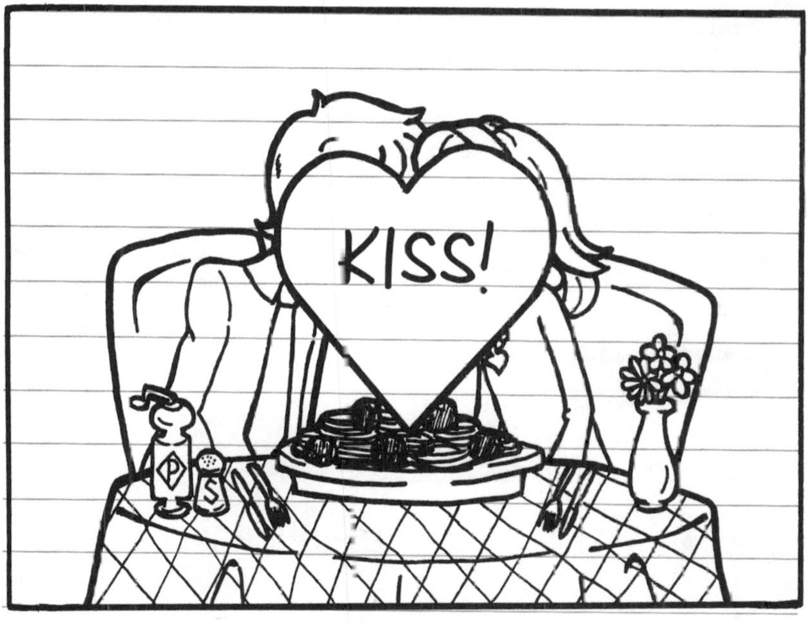
KISS!

SQUEEE ☺!! Hey! It could actually happen!! Hmmm . . . I wonder how much private lessons with a figure skating coach cost . . . ?

ME, AS A GRACEFUL ICE PRINCESS TRAINING WITH MY COACH!

FRIDAY, DECEMBER 20

Today is the last day of school! This means I'm officially on winter break! WOO-HOO ☺!

Christmas is my most favorite holiday! WHY?!

Because you get lots of presents AND a long vacation from school! It's like having a birthday and a mini summer vacation all rolled into one.

How cool is THAT?!

The only downside is that by the time you hit middle school, most parents really start slacking off on their gift-giving responsibilities.

Every year I get the same old cruddy gifts—pajamas, socks, fruitcake, and an electric toothbrush with no batteries in it (DUH!).

I'm so DISGUSTED! I have such a large inventory of cheap, junky gifts I could actually open my own DOLLAR STORE or something. . . .

But THIS year is going to be different! And yes, it was probably a little tacky of me to "accidentally" leave copies of my wish list plastered all over the house for Mom to find. . . .

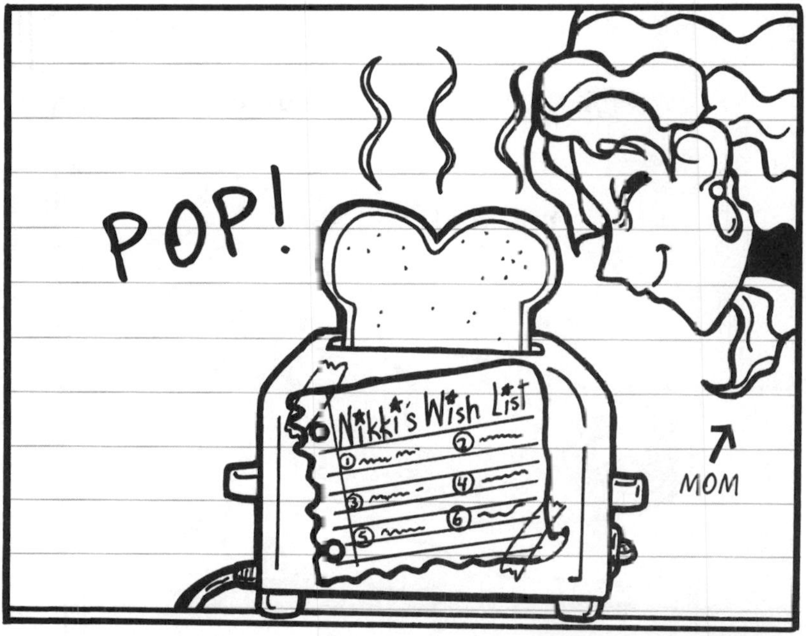
POP!
Nikki's Wish List
MOM

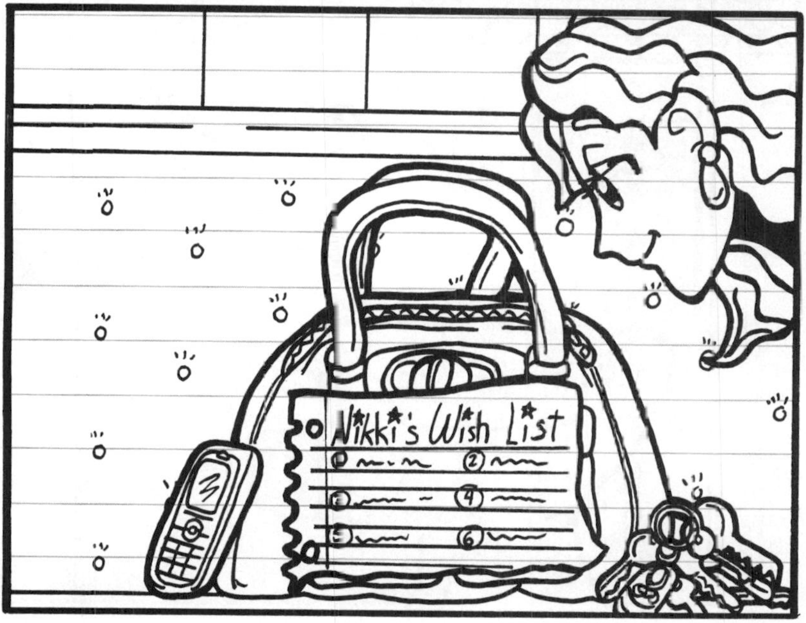
Nikki's Wish List

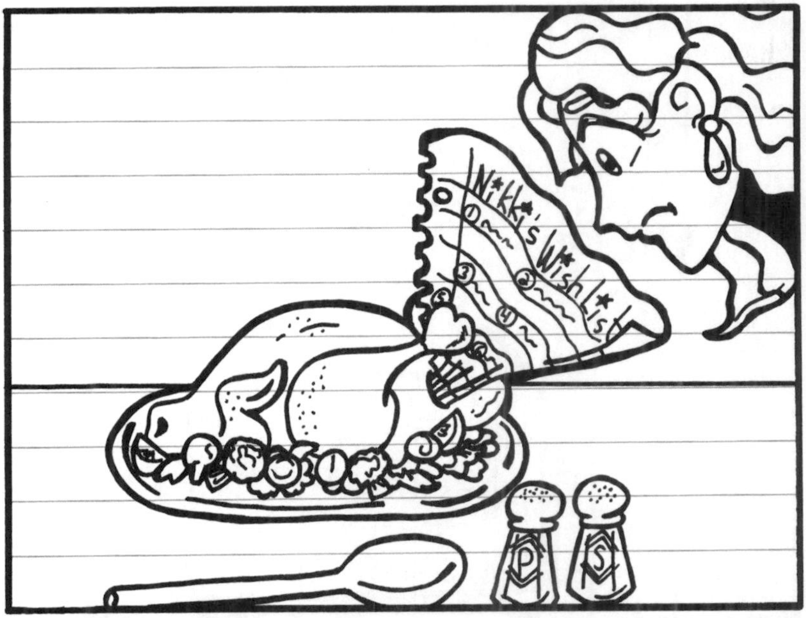
Nikki's Wish List
P
S

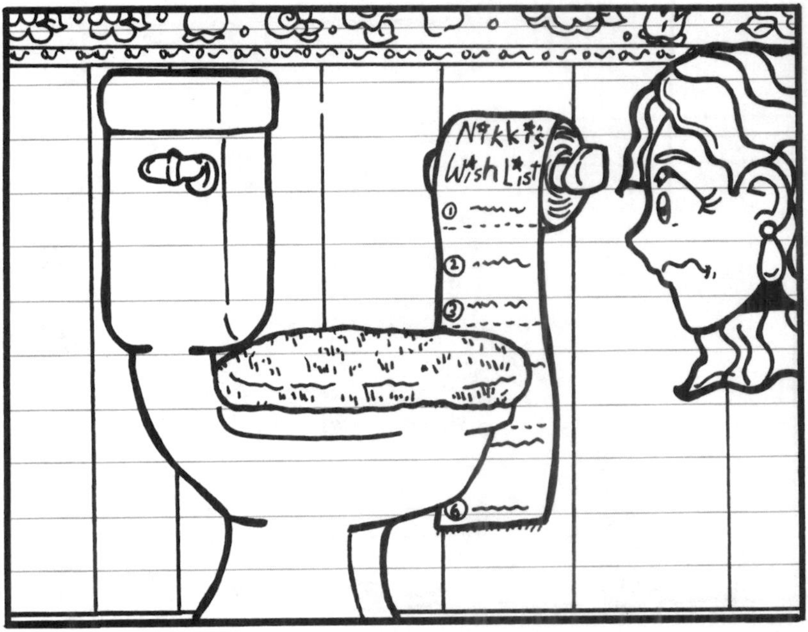
Nikki's Wish List

I'm sure my wish list was way more exciting reading than those dusty old *Reader's Digests* my dad keeps in the bathroom.

Anyway, when Mom announced that she had not just ONE, but TWO early Christmas presents for Brianna and me to open—I was pleasantly shocked and surprised.

Had I known my brilliant, in—your—face marketing strategy was going to work so well, I would have used it years ago.

The larger present was SO big, I guessed that it probably contained my new laptop computer, cell phone, art supplies, AND cash.

"I hope it's a chocolate cake!" Brianna screamed excitedly. "I'm going to have a Princess Sugar Plum chocolate cake for my birthday!"

We both ripped open our gift at the same time. I almost FAINTED when I saw what was inside. . . .

"MOM!! WHAT THE . . . ?!!
A PRINCESS SUGAR PLUM DRESS?!"

Apparently, Mom had paid our neighbor lady,
Mrs. Wallabanger, to make us these sickeningly

frilly MATCHING Princess Sugar Plum dresses.

Then Mom got all emotional and teary-eyed.

"Girls, the best part is that tomorrow you'll be wearing these beautiful dresses to a VERY special event!"

I was like, "Mom! Are you KA-RAY-ZEE??!!"

But I just said that inside my head, so no one else heard it but me.

I hoped that the event was going to be at a junkyard, an abandoned parking garage, a cow pasture, or a sewage treatment plant. Anywhere there'd be a limited number of life-forms to see me in that UGLY dress!

Mom giggled and begged us to open our second present. Judging from the very small size, I was hoping it was a box of matches.

Then I'd be able to BURN my new dress in the fireplace. But no such luck ☹!

"SURPRISE!! For Family Sharing Time, we're going to see the *Nutcracker* ballet!" Mom exclaimed.

I was SO frustrated I wanted to scream!

"AAAAAHHHHH!"

WHY was my mom giving me an UGLY dress and a BORING ballet theater ticket, when I've been BEGGING for a new CELL PHONE for, like, FOREVER?!

Had she not even BOTHERED to READ the twenty-seven copies of my wish list that I had discreetly left lying around the house?!

Hey, if I'm gonna watch a stage show, it better include slammin' vocals, krazy-good dancers, special effects, fireworks, loud guitar solos, and crowd surfing.

I am so NOT looking forward to this.

If Mom really wants to TORTURE me, she should just make me stay home and BABYSIT BRIANNA while blasting Dad's LAME disco music until my EARS BLEED.

I'm just saying . . .

☹!!

I just stared at myself in the mirror in total disbelief.

How was this possible?

I HATED that hideous dress even MORE than I did yesterday.

I decided it was time to take legal action. I was going to sue my parents.

For CRUELTY to children!

"Girls! It's time to go!" Mom chirped cheerfully. "I can't wait to see how beautiful the two of you look!"

I adjusted the huge bow in my hair, which was the size of a small seagull.

I looked just like one of those creepy Victorian porcelain dolls you find in antique shops.

ME, AS A VERY
CREEPY VICTORIAN
PORCELAIN DOLL

To make matters
worse, the fancy
shoes were killing
my feet. I so
wanted to wear
my worn-out
sneakers.

It was going to
be painful enough
to have to sit
through a
two-hour
SNOOZEFEST.

Hey, I might
as well have
comfy feet.

Brianna, Mom, and I wore red dresses and matching

bows, while Dad wore a black suit with a red shirt and a big red-and-white polka-dotted bow tie.

I caught a glimpse of the four of us in the living room mirror and actually had a mini meltdown.

We looked like a family of, um . . . CIRCUS CLOWNS . . . all dressed up for a . . . clown . . . FUNERAL or something!

All we needed now was . . .

1. Some rubber balls for Dad

2. One of those trick plastic flowers that squirt water for Mom

3. A big plastic horn for Brianna, AND

4. A little clown car for me, so I can jump in and drive away from my crazy family.

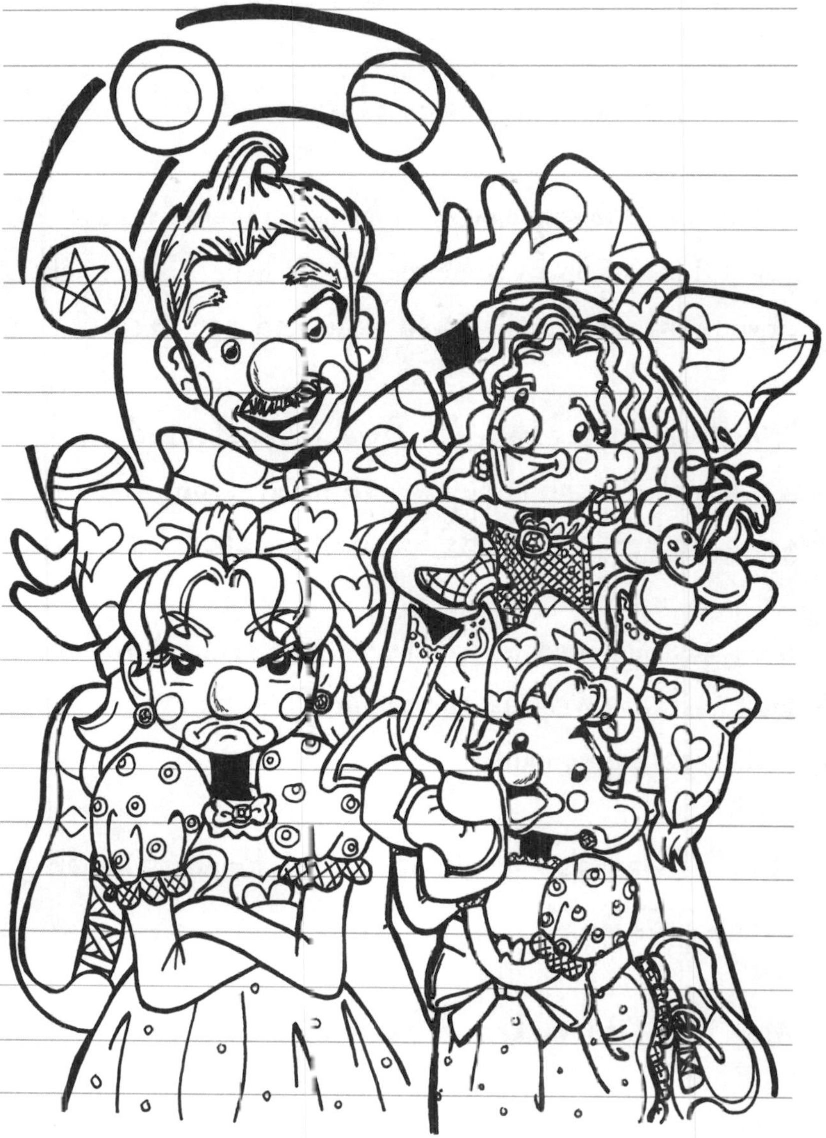

CLOWNS "R" US!

For some reason, Brianna's dress fit a little strangely.

Probably because it was on backward. DUH!

"Brianna," Mom groaned. "I knew I shouldn't have let you put that on by yourself. Come here." She knelt down next to Brianna and adjusted her dress.

"No! I can dress myself!" Brianna protested. "I'm a big girl! My birthday is coming up soon, and I'm going to get a Princess Sugar Plum chocolate cake."

Mom just ignored her. "There," she said. "Now you look just as lovely as the Sugar Plum Fairy. She'll be in the ballet tonight."

"Hey!" Brianna's eyes lit up. "Is she Princess Sugar Plum's SISTER?"

Mom and Dad winked at each other.

"It's very possible," Mom said. "We're going to see her and her ballerina friends dance in pretty costumes. It's going to be a lot of fun. You'll see."

"Nikki, tell me the story about Princess Sugar Plum's sister? Please!" Brianna begged.

I rolled my eyes. It was a complicated story. And Brianna had the attention span of a Tater Tot.

"Well, her friend Clara gets a lame toy, her brother breaks it, it comes to life, their house gets infested with dancing rats, and they visit a land full of candy and desserts. Then their world gets taken over by an evil Rat King," I muttered.

"CANDY and DESSERTS?!" Brianna squealed, basically ignoring everything I'd said about doom, gloom, and dancing rodents. "Do you think there's chocolate cake there?"

"There's every dessert you can imagine," Mom added dreamily. "The flowers, trees, and castles are all made of sweets. Doesn't that sound amazing?"

We all piled into the car, and about thirty minutes later we arrived at this huge, swanky-looking theater. Everyone there had on suits and formal dresses.

Mom had managed to get us seats really close to the stage so we'd have a good view. But guess who got stuck sitting next to Brianna?

ME!!

I think Mom and Dad did that on purpose, because while the orchestra was warming up, they left their seats to go chat with friends.

I mean, WHO did they think I was? Mary Poppins?! Nanny McPhee?!

While Brianna and I were sitting there, she suddenly started swinging her feet and kicking the seat in front of us while singing a superobnoxious song she'd made up:

"Sugar plums, cookies, and candy
But watch out, Mr. Rat
'Cause if you touch my chocolate cake
I'll whack you with a bat!"

An older man wearing a tux turned around and gave us BOTH a dirty look.

Which made no sense whatsoever because I wasn't the one singing and kicking his seat!

"Brianna," I hissed, "stop kicking that man's seat. And please be quiet!"

"Hi, Mr. Bald Guy! How did you get your head to shine like that? Guess what? I'm wearing a new dress. On my birthday I'm going to get a chocolate—"

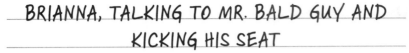

BRIANNA, TALKING TO MR. BALD GUY AND KICKING HIS SEAT

"Brianna! Zip it!" I snapped.

Finally Mom and Dad came back to their seats and the theater lights dimmed.

But Brianna was already bored out of her skull.

When the orchestra started playing, she must have decided it was the perfect music for her little song because she started singing at the top of her lungs:

> "Sugar plums, cookies, and candy
> But watch out, Mr. Rat—"

"Shhh!" At least a dozen frowning people shushed her.

I sank down in my seat and pretended I was with another family.

That's when Mom shot us BOTH a Death Stare.

Which made no sense whatsoever.

I wasn't the one singing about a RAT, really loudly and off-key.

All throughout the first act Brianna squirmed and kicked the seat in front of her.

But at least she was quiet.

Thank goodness.

Until the evil Rat King and his minions appeared.

That's when Brianna stood up in her chair, pointed at the stage, and screamed:

"Holy McNuggets! Those dancing rats are HUGE! And guess what?! My sister had a Halloween costume like that! Didn't you, Nikki? Except yours was really stinky . . . !"

BRIANNA, SCREAMING AT THE RATS

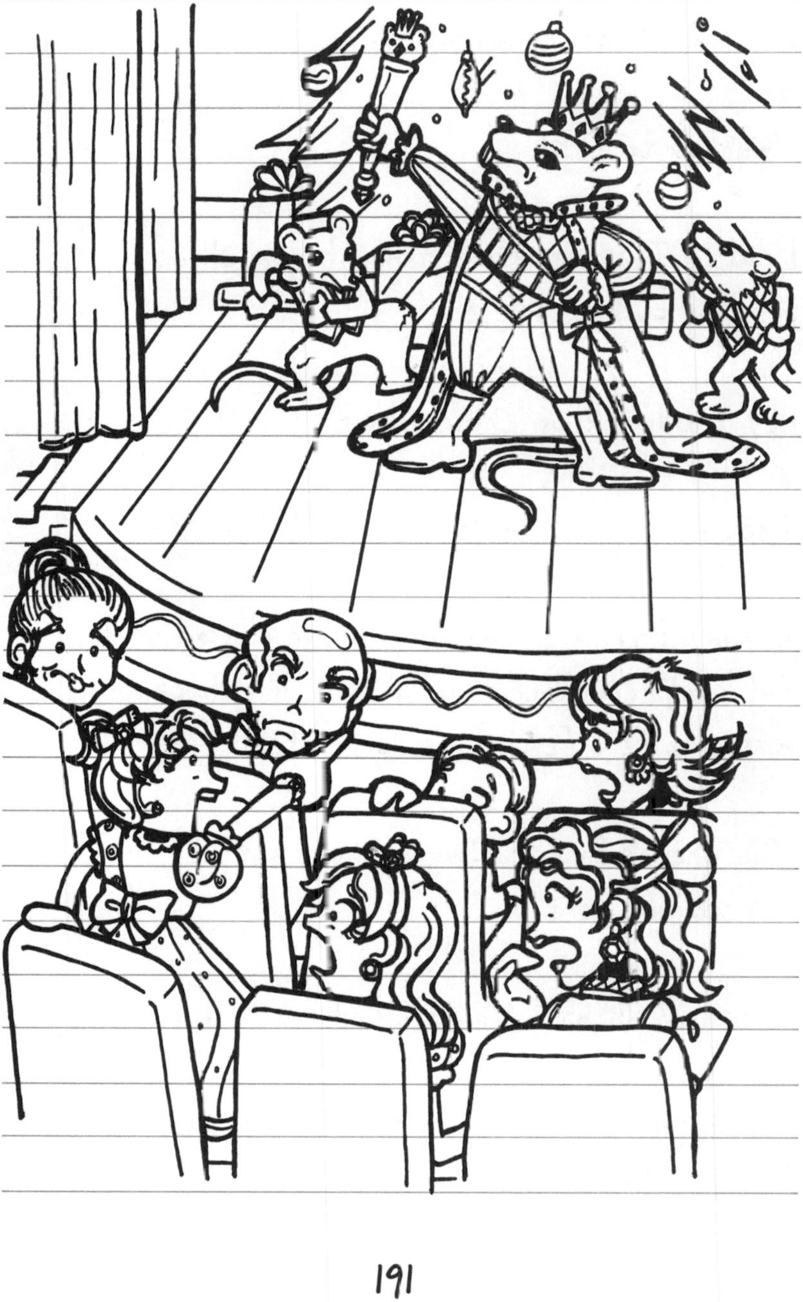
WAH!

Everyone turned and shot us dirty looks.

OMG! I was SO embarrassed.

I wanted to DIE!

I did NOT appreciate Brianna telling all of my personal business like that.

Hey, I didn't know those people.

They were, like, complete . . . STRANGERS!

Anyway, I think Brianna must have messed up the Rat King's concentration or something because he missed quite a few of his dance steps.

"So, where's Princess Sugar Plum's sister?" Brianna blurted out next.

"Brianna! Shhhh!" Mom scolded her in a whisper.

"Nikki, please try to keep your sister quiet, okay?" Dad pleaded under his breath.

"I am. She's just NOT listening!" I huffed kind of loudly.

Oops. I forgot to use my "inside" voice.

"SHHHHHHHH!!" At least a dozen people shushed me.

Finally the curtains came down and the lights went on for intermission.

OMG! It seemed like the entire audience was staring at us all evil-like.

"This is why you don't bring children to the theater," the bald guy in the tux muttered loudly to his wife, followed by a few not-so-nice words.

Brianna tapped him on his shoulder again.

"Hey, Mr. Baldy! Did you see those huge rats up on that stage?! Boy, were they scary!"

That was the last straw for the tux guy.

He turned beet red, stood up, stomped over to an usher, and demanded that he and his wife be given new seats.

I wanted to grab hold of his coattails, drop to my knees, and beg desperately, "Please, sir, take me with you. Please!"

I had to get a break from Brianna before I totally lost it.

"I'll be right back!" I said to my parents. "I'm going to find some water. Or a ride home, if I'm lucky."

"Wait, Nikki! I wanna go toooo!" Brianna whined.

"I'll be right back, Brianna."

"But I need to go to the bathroom!"

"Nikki, could you take your sister to the bathroom? Please?" Mom asked.

DARN IT!!

I wanted to argue with Mom. But if Brianna had an accident while we were discussing the matter, I knew Mom was going to blame me.

And I was pretty sure the concessions stand DIDN'T sell Pampers in her size.

"Come on, Brianna!" I grumped.

"Thank you, dear!" Mom smiled. "I appreciate it."

Once we got to the bathroom, I tried my best to be patient with Brianna.

"Now, hurry up and go, okay? The show will be starting again soon, and we want to get back to our seats before they dim the lights."

"Don't rush me!" Brianna said, and stuck her tongue out at me.

As she walked into the stall her eyes lit up. . . .

HEY, LOOK AT ALL OF THIS TOILET PAPER!

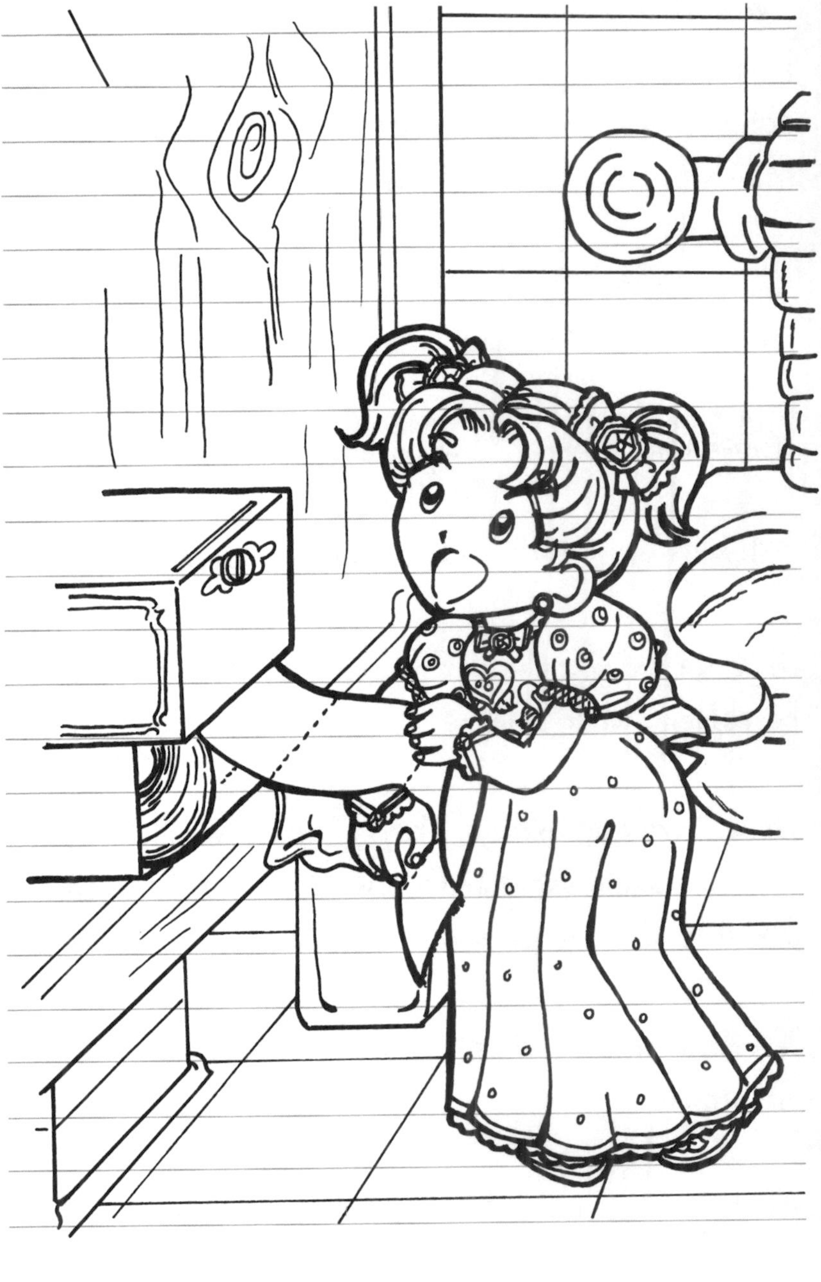

"Oh, goody! Now I can pretend my arm is broken and wrap it up," she squealed happily.

Just great! I sighed.

This was going to take FOREVER!

I waited for three long minutes.

"Brianna, are you done yet?"

"Almost. Now I'm wrapping up my broken head."

"Your broken WHAT?! Brianna, let's GO! NOW!"

"But I STILL have to use the BATHROOM!"

"Fine! I'll be waiting for you on that bench right outside the bathroom door. When you get done, wash your hands and come right out. Okay?"

"Okay! Um, Nikki, do you have any . . . glue?"

I made a mental note-to-self: If, during my

lifetime, Mom EVER asks me to take Brianna to the bathroom again, run away SCREAMING!

I hadn't been sitting on the bench for more than a minute when I noticed a long line of people waiting to buy these huge gourmet cupcakes in a fancy glass display case on the other side of the lobby.

I guess Brianna's obsessive rambling about chocolate cake must have affected my subconscious or something.

Because I could almost hear the double-fudge chocolate cupcakes calling my name.

Soon the line had dwindled down to two people, and Brianna was still nowhere in sight.

That's when I decided to make a mad dash to buy a cupcake.

It wasn't my fault that by taking Brianna to the bathroom I had worked up a tremendous appetite.

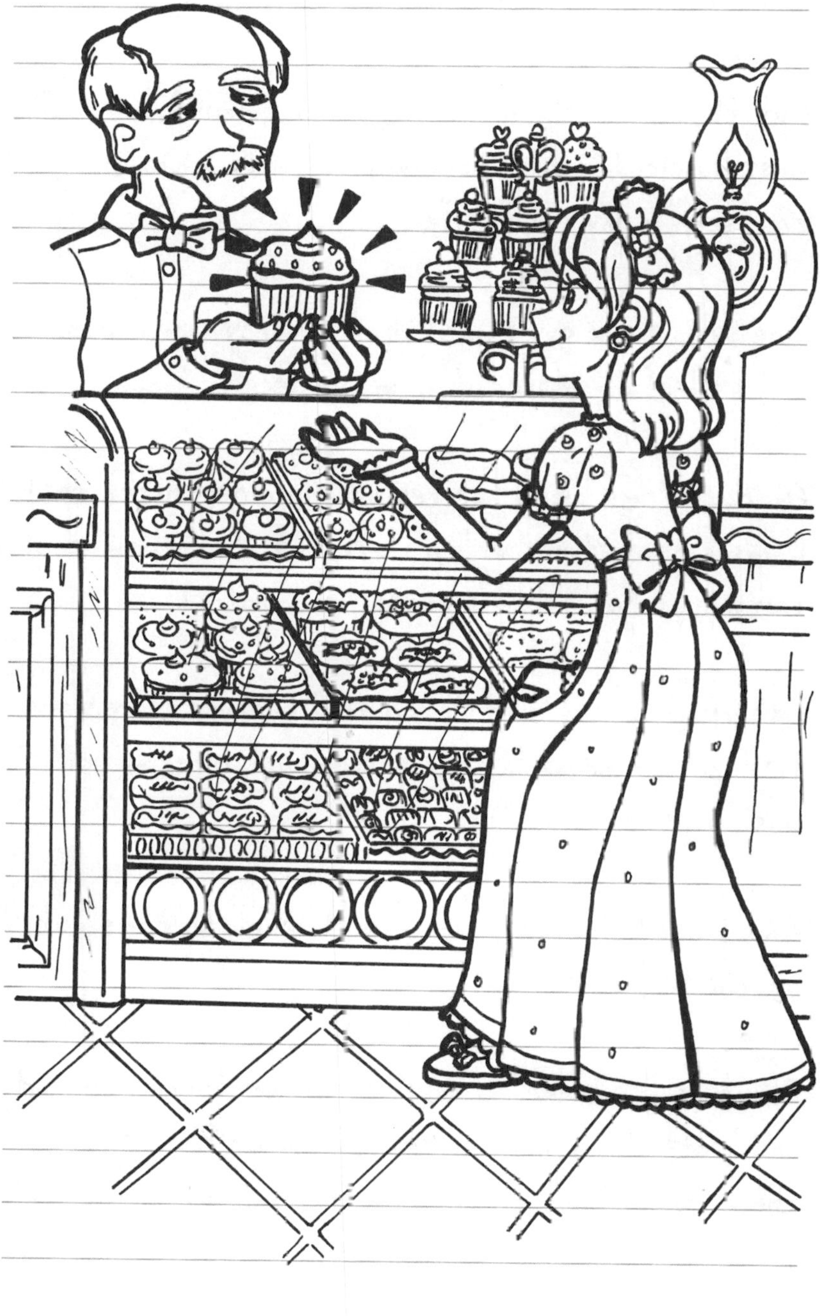

They were way overpriced at $7.00 each.

But they were the most—large, most—moist, most—luscious, most—chocolaty cupcakes I had ever seen in my entire life.

The sales clerk guy placed it in a fancy white box, and I carefully placed it in my purse.

Of course, me being the responsible older sister that I was, I never took my eyes off that bathroom door for more than a few seconds (or minutes).

I started to get a little worried because they were flashing the house lights, which meant intermission was about to end.

And I was STILL waiting for Brianna to come out of the bathroom.

So you can imagine my surprise when I turned around and spotted a frilly red Princess Sugar Plum dress at the drinking fountain on the other side of the lobby.

I rushed right over.

"There you are, Brianna! You were in the bathroom FOREVER! We need to get back to our seats right now. Come on!"

I grabbed her hand and pulled her through the lobby.

That's when she stared up at me with the most HORRIFIED look on her face.

My brain was STILL trying to figure out how Brianna had gotten curly red hair, freckles, and glasses.

But my mouth came up with the answer and suddenly blurted . . .

"Hey! You're NOT Brianna!"

"Mommy!" the little girl cried. "Stranger danger! Stranger danger!"

ME, WITH A LITTLE GIRL WHO IS APPARENTLY *NOT BRIANNA*

NOT ACTUALLY BRIANNA

Startled, I dropped her hand and backed away.

"My bad!" I apologized. "I thought you were someone else! Sorry!"

Then I rushed back to the bathroom to try to find my little sister.

"Brianna? Are you in here? Brianna!" I screamed as I checked every stall. But she was nowhere to be found.

My heart started to pound and my palms got really sweaty. I frantically ran back out into the hall and scanned the lobby. Still no Brianna.

That's when I started to panic. OMG! What if she's lost FOREVER?! The terrifying thought overwhelmed me.

I couldn't imagine life without my little sister, even though she was a Category 5 hurricane in pigtails.

I was so distraught, I even started to miss Miss Penelope.

I vowed that if I found Brianna, I'd buy a new purple pen and personally give Miss Penelope a glamorous makeover.

But now I had to go back into that theater and tell Mom and Dad I had somehow lost Brianna. I was ~~hoping~~ PRAYING Brianna had just wandered back into the auditorium.

If only she was back in her seat, safe and sound, torturing the people sitting nearby by kicking their seats, singing her obnoxious little song, and chatting with Mr. Baldy.

The ballet had already started up again by the time I got to my row. This meant I had to crawl over about a dozen highly annoyed people.

"Excuse me. I need to get through. Was that your foot? Sorry! I apologize. Oops!"

By the time I got to my seat, my eyes were finally starting to adjust to the darkness. I fully expected to see Brianna come into focus at any second.

"What took you so long?" Mom whispered really loudly. "We were starting to worry! Um, Nikki, dear . . . WHERE'S BRIANNA?!!"

I opened my mouth, but at first no words came out.

"She's not here? I thought maybe she came back to her seat!"

Mom's expression shifted from curiosity to alarm.

"WHAT?!" she said even louder.

Of course, everyone shot her dirty looks.

"I—I was waiting for her in the bathroom, and she just . . . VANISHED!"

"Did you check all the stalls?"

"YES! Three times."

"Uh, dear . . ." Dad tapped Mom's arm nervously. His eyes were frozen on the stage.

"How about the lobby and the concessions stand?" Mom continued. "Maybe she saw some candy."

"Mom, I looked EVERYWHERE!"

"Well, let's not panic. Maybe she's playing in the elevators. Let's go back out to the lobby and—"

"DEAR, you REALLY need to see this!" Dad interrupted again.

"What could possibly be more important right now than trying to find . . ."

That's when Mom and I looked up at the stage. "BRIANNA!!" we both screamed.

Clara and the Nutcracker prince were making their grand entrance to the Land of Sweets in an extravagant boat.

With a little stowaway in the backseat. Who was festively draped in what looked like a full roll of toilet paper.

"Brianna!" Mom called out to her.

But either Brianna couldn't hear Mom or she was ignoring her.

Brianna seemed almost hypnotized by the candy cane trees, gumdrop bushes, and the humongous cupcake castle on the stage.

But the really scary part was that she had this mischievous grin that went from ear to ear.

The confused audience immediately noticed Brianna onstage in her toilet-paper outfit.

Most of them scratched their heads and whispered to each other.

No one seemed to remember there being a pint-sized mummy in *The Nutcracker*.

Clara and the Nutcracker prince, still all smiles, stared back at the audience with perplexed looks on their faces.

But when they finally turned and saw Brianna
standing there smiling and waving at the audience,
they totally FREAKED. . . .

BRIANNA

Clara frantically whispered something to the prince.

He then leaned over, picked up Brianna, and tried to carry her off the stage. But Brianna stubbornly held on to the boat for dear life. Finally he gave up and just left her there.

When the dancers took the stage, they didn't notice Brianna right away either.

Some of them were dressed as cookies, and others as candy. Then came the dancing chefs holding trays of pies, cupcakes, and assorted pastries.

"That's what I'm talking 'bout!" Brianna screamed, and jumped out of the boat.

She bolted for the dancers like a crazy bull.

Mom, Dad, and I ran toward the stage as fast as we could.

The moment felt surreal and like we were moving in slow motion.

"BRIANNA!" Mom cried. "NOOOOO!"

But there was no way we could get there before she started her feeding frenzy.

First, she grabbed a male dancer by the ankle and bit into his chocolate boot.

She made a face. "Yuck! That's NOT chocolate!"

The dancer shook her off his leg.

Next, Brianna ran to a candy ballerina and grabbed her tutu.

The ballerina stopped dancing and tugged back.

But a piece of her tutu ripped off in Brianna's hand, and Brianna shoved it into her mouth. "Eww!" She spat it out and frowned. "That's NOT cotton candy!"

Almost all the characters stopped dancing and scrambled off the stage to avoid being eaten alive. Soon the only dancer left was a clueless chef

carrying a huge chocolate cake. He was totally
focused on executing a series of grand pliés.

"Run! Run!" the frenzied audience chanted excitedly.

I couldn't believe it!

I expected people would be walking out, booing, or at least throwing rotten veggies.

But their butts were glued to their seats, and their eyes to the stage like they were watching the last ten minutes of a Super Bowl game and the score was tied.

Brianna spotted the huge cake and just stared at it in awe.

When the chef finally caught a glimpse of Brianna, he suddenly stopped dancing and looked like he was about to wet his pants!

Brianna ran across the stage and lunged for the chef like a football player making a tackle.

The chef screamed, threw the chocolate cake up in the air, and dove into the orchestra pit.

There was a crash and a loud, off-key note from the tuba.

It was quite obvious what musician the dancing chef had landed on.

Brianna triumphantly grabbed the cake and took a huge bite out of it just as we made it to the stage.

"Brianna, you come down here this instant!" Mom ordered.

Brianna lifted her head from the cake.

Her face was smeared with chocolate frosting, and her mouth was so full she looked like a blowfish.

After chewing for a few seconds, she frowned.

Perplexed and disappointed, Brianna pointed at the fake pastry. "Thith isn'th thocolate cake!" she said.

I barely made out what she was saying, but I saw
white Styrofoam where she'd bitten a huge chunk
out of the cake.

"There's no real food up here. It's all just props," I
scolded. "I can't believe you did this!"

"Iz this a joke? Noth funny!" She pouted.

"Brianna Lynn Maxwell!" Mom shouted, and gave her the Death Stare. "Don't make me come up there . . . !"

Uh-oh! Mom meant business.

"Yeth, ma'am," Brianna finally mumbled in defeat.

She spat out the faux cake and jumped from the stage into Mom's arms.

Then the most shocking thing happened.

The dancers, the orchestra, AND the audience gave Mom a standing ovation for single-handedly bringing the *Nutcracker* catastrophe to an end.

And get this!

After Brianna had pretty much obliterated the *Nutcracker* ballet, she actually had the nerve to wave and blow kisses to everyone, like she was on that *Toddlers & Tiaras* show or something.

I felt a lot better when a ten-minute intermission was announced so the dancers could prepare to start the second act over again.

And then the house lights came on.

As we left the theater the audience was still laughing and cheering for Brianna, including Mr. Baldy.

It was hard to believe those stuffy folks actually loved the *Nutcracker* ballet as a slapstick comedy.

We piled into the car and rode home in silence.

Mostly because no one had the energy to lecture Brianna.

If she had been MY child, I would have dropped her off at the nearest mental hospital for a psychiatric evaluation.

Or, better yet, the city zoo.

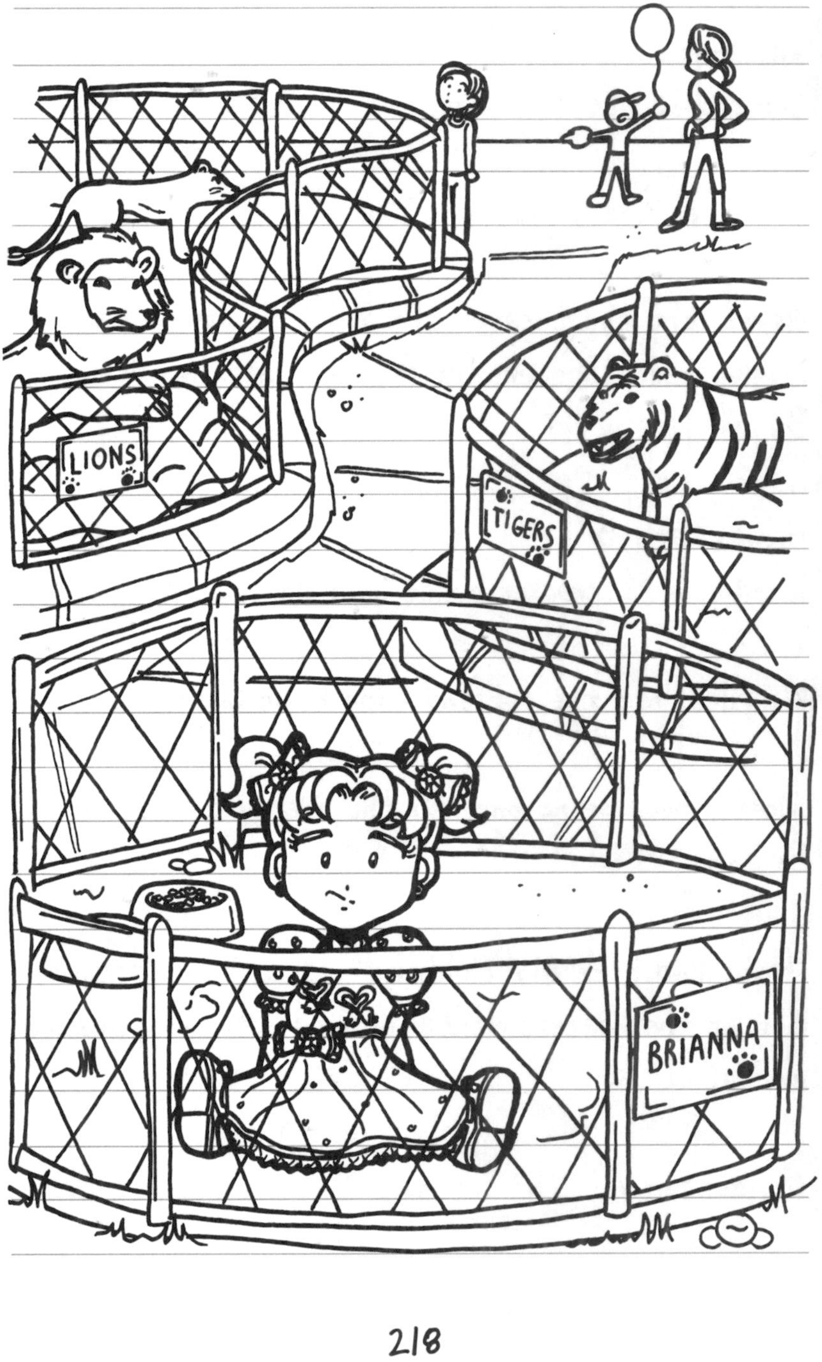
LIONS
TIGERS
BRIANNA

But she WASN'T my child. Thank goodness!

Even though I wanted to be angry at Brianna, deep down I was happy and relieved that she was okay.

It felt good to be home again. But my poor mom and dad were so exhausted they went straight to bed.

Being the responsible older daughter that I am, I assured my parents I would see to it that Brianna got into her pj's and safely tucked in.

I was surprised that she didn't whine and complain like she usually does at bedtime. She just hung her head, trudged upstairs, and changed into her SpongeBob pajamas.

I felt kind of sorry for her. In a way, all of this was mostly our fault. We had overemphasized the whole sugary-dessert theme of *The Nutcracker*.

Brianna was just a little kid. How was she supposed to know all the scenery and the chocolate cake was fake?

That's when I suddenly remembered MY cupcake, and my mouth started to water all over again.

I rushed downstairs to pour myself a tall, cold glass of milk.

I couldn't wait to get back to my room and sink my teeth into that luscious chocolaty cupcake while I wrote in my diary.

When I passed Brianna's room, I could tell she was still pretty upset. Even with her door closed, I could hear her sniffling and muttering to herself.

However, I froze in my tracks when I heard her sing what had to be the saddest song EVER:

"No sugar plums, cookies, or candy
The cupcake castle was flat
The chocolate cake was really fake
Sometimes I'm . . . such a . . . BRAT!"

I carefully placed my cupcake and glass of milk on the floor in front of her door. . . .

Then I knocked on her door.

By the time Brianna opened it, I'd already dashed to my room and flopped across my bed.

I heard her squeal in delight!

"CHOCOLATE CAKE?! Thank you, Princess Sugar Plum! You made my WISH come true!"

"You're welcome!" I said aloud to myself, and smiled.

Who would have thunk this night would turn out so well?

Brianna DIDN'T end up on the side of a milk carton as a missing child.

The audience seemed to enjoy her antics in that wacky comedy-ballet-reality show.

And Mom and Dad were too exhausted to ground me for the rest of my life for losing Brianna.

But most important, I discovered that giving away something you cherish to someone you love can actually make you happier than keeping it.

I guess that's what the holidays are all about.

Oh, crud! I think I'm starting to sound like one of Mom's sappy greeting cards.

Hmmm, maybe my family isn't so BAD after all.

NOT!! ☺!!

ME, GIVING MY KOOKY
← FAMILY A BIG HUG!

When we got home from church this morning, it was snowing like crazy. And by noon we had gotten a total of four inches.

As far as I was concerned, it was the perfect weather to curl up in front of the fireplace and sip hot cocoa with marshmallows.

But NOOO! My parents FORCED me to go outside in near-blizzard conditions for the STUPIDEST reason.

They wanted to build a snowman for Brianna!

Mom got all excited and said it would be a wonderful project for Family Sharing Time. But I already knew it was going to be a major DISASTER.

It was Dad's bright idea to make a life-size snowman. He was off to a really good start as his snowball grew bigger and bigger and bigger.

Then, unfortunately, he lost control of it on a hill. . . .

Well, there was good news and bad news.

The GOOD news was that Brianna ended up with a life-size snowman just like Dad had promised her.

But the BAD news was that DAD was the life-size snowman.

After he ran down that big hill, he dived headfirst into this huge snowbank. Then his snowball landed right on top of him. CRUNCH!!

OMG!! It took us ten minutes just to dig him out.

And by the time we got to him, he had NEW frostbite on top of the OLD frostbite he'd gotten from the snowblower fiasco.

I felt SO sorry for him. Especially since he was run over by that snowball while trying to do something nice for Brianna.

I just hope Dad isn't traumatized and suffering from some weird illness like snowman-a-phobia.

At this point, I don't think we're going to be building any more snowmen anytime soon.

Thank goodness!

Which allows me even MORE free time to curl up in front of the fireplace, drink hot cocoa with marshmallows, and write in my DIARY.

I almost forgot! I STILL need to go shopping and buy a few more presents.

I've decided to give Brandon a Christmas present too. He's SUCH a sweetheart!

I just have to figure out something he'd really like.

Hmmm. Maybe a gift certificate for a romantic spaghetti dinner for TWO at Giovanni's!

SQUEEEE!!

☺!!

Every year, I wait until the very last minute to do my Christmas shopping. I sneak out of the house with Brianna, and we ride my bike in the snow to the nearest drugstore. . . .

Since I don't have my driver's license yet, we're basically forced to shop at the closest place we can get to before we catch PNEUMONIA.

That's why Mom and Dad always get tacky presents, like a family-size pack of toothbrushes from me and gummy vitamins from Brianna.

"GIRLS!! YOU SHOULDN'T HAVE!!"

But this year I wanted to get them something special that they'd REALLY like.

You know, in addition to the toothbrushes and vitamins.

I was SO happy when I saw this huge bin of scrapbooks on sale!

It was BUY ONE, GET FOUR FREE! I was really lucky to stumble upon such a great holiday sale.

Or maybe the store was just trying to pawn them off on unsuspecting customers so there'd be less junk to throw away at the end of the shopping season.

Anyway, seeing those scrapbooks really got my creative juices flowing.

I decided to buy one as a gift for Mom and Dad. I planned to use my advanced skills in arts and crafts to create a beautiful new cover. It would be PERFECT for our family photos.

And since I was getting four extra scrapbooks
for FREE, I decided to give one to Chloe, Zoey,
Brianna, and Brandon, too.

Was I not BRILLIANT ☺?!

I'd make Chloe and Zoey each a special scrapbook
about our friendship.

And I knew Brianna would love anything with Princess
Sugar Plum on the cover.

But then I started thinking about Brandon. What if
he actually ended up moving away?

I wanted to give him something to remind him of our
friendship and all the fun times we'd had.

Like the art competition, the Halloween party,
and the talent show. And even that time I actually
thought I'd lost my diary at school!

Suddenly I started feeling really sad, right there in
the Cold, Flu & Allergy medicine aisle.

I really wanted to help Brandon by skating in the *Holiday on Ice* show.

But I was also scared to death that I couldn't pull it off.

If only I could find someone to skate in my place!

I sighed and tried to swallow the huge lump in my throat.

Sometimes it felt like I was carrying the weight of the world on my shoulders.

Just as I was about to go through the checkout, I saw a familiar face in the lip gloss section of the cosmetics aisle.

It was MACKENZIE!!

My heart skipped a beat! Maybe there was hope for Brandon after all. If I put aside my ego and simply ~~asked~~ BEGGED her for help, maybe she would consider skating in my place.

"OMG! Hi, MacKenzie! I didn't know you shopped here," I said all friendlylike.

She looked at me and scowled. "Nikki, what are YOU doing here? Why aren't you hanging out with your dorky little friends at McTacoHut or somewhere?" she said.

I was dreading our conversation would go like this. But it was my fault. I should have appealed to her huge ego and opened with flattery.

"I absolutely love your lip gloss. The color brings out the highlights in your eyes," I gushed.

"Well, you should try that new peachy color. It'll complement your mustache hairs."

I could NOT believe she said that right to my face.

"Hey, I've seen PIGS wear lip gloss and look better than you!" I muttered under my breath.

"WHAT did you just say?!" she snapped.

We stared at each other. It was SO AWKWARD!

I needed her help so I lied through my teeth. "I said, 'Hey! I see PINK lip gloss looks good on YOU.'"

"Um, why are you even talking to me, Nikki?"

"Well, it's about *Holiday on Ice*. I know you wanted to skate for Fuzzy Friends. And now I'm having second thoughts."

"You're actually having thoughts? I'm impressed."

I just ignored her comment.

"MacKenzie, I want to ask you a big favor?"

"What? A donation to your plastic-surgery fund for the removal of mustache hair?"

I ignored THAT comment too.

"Would you take my place and skate with Zoey and Chloe for *Holiday on Ice*? We really need that money to keep Fuzzy Friends open."

"I'm surprised you didn't just ask me."

"I've wanted to ask you since last week. You're one of the best skaters in the show. If I mess this up, Brandon will be crushed. And it'll all be my fault."

MacKenzie looked amused and smiled. "YES! You're absolutely correct!" she said.

"OMG! Is that a YES, you'll skate for me?" I exclaimed happily.

I could NOT believe MacKenzie had actually said yes! It was a MIRACLE!

"NO! That's a YES, that Brandon will be CRUSHED and it will be YOUR fault! Sorry, Nikki! But if you were on FIRE, I wouldn't SPIT on you!"

"What about Brandon? Then at least do it for him. If anything happens to Fuzzy Friends, he's going to be heartbroken!"

"I know!" she said smugly. "Actually, I'm counting on

it! WHO is going to be there for Brandon when he needs a shoulder to cry on after his STUPID little shelter closes? ME! That's who! And the best part is that he's going to HATE YOU for letting him down. And that's just the way I want it!"

Then MacKenzie cackled like a witch.

I just stood there in SHOCK!!

I could not believe anything breathing could be that EVIL.

It's quite obvious that MacKenzie has set me up! AGAIN!! I'm SO sick of her little mind games!

But I'm NOT going to get MAD!

I'm going to get EVEN!

By believing in myself and skating my BUTT off!

And I'm going to be STRONG! And FIERCE! And, of course, wear a SUPERCUTE outfit!

I'll be more deadly than that Terminator guy.

I'm going to be . . .

THE SKATER-NATOR

ME →

Anyway, all the scrapbooks I made turned out really cute.

And the pages Brianna decorated for Mom and Dad were, um . . . quite . . . interesting.

Me, Nikki ♥

Brianna and Dad at Camp Caring.

Brianna as the Easter Bunny.

Love

I plan to wrap all the scrapbooks and then deliver Chloe's and Zoey's on Christmas Eve.

I decided to just leave Brandon's in the mailbox at Fuzzy Friends since he spends so much time there anyway.

I think he's going to be supersurprised I actually made a special gift for him.

Now he'll have a special place to keep all his photos.

I just hope he likes it.

☺!

Today is Christmas Eve!

One of Mom's favorite winter craft projects is knitting matching sweaters for our family.

This year it's a fairly hideous snowman sweater with a string of plastic ornaments trimming the collar.

The sweater is blue and has one red sleeve, one green sleeve, and a huge 3-D snowman on the front.

Our names were knitted in six-inch yellow letters across the back.

I thought about sending mine off to *Guinness World Records* as an entry for Ugliest Sweater in the History of Mankind.

I didn't care about setting a record. I just wanted to get rid of the darn thing before someone actually made me wear it. But it was too late. . . .

HEY, HONEY! LET'S TAKE A FAMILY PICTURE IN THESE PRETTY SWEATERS!

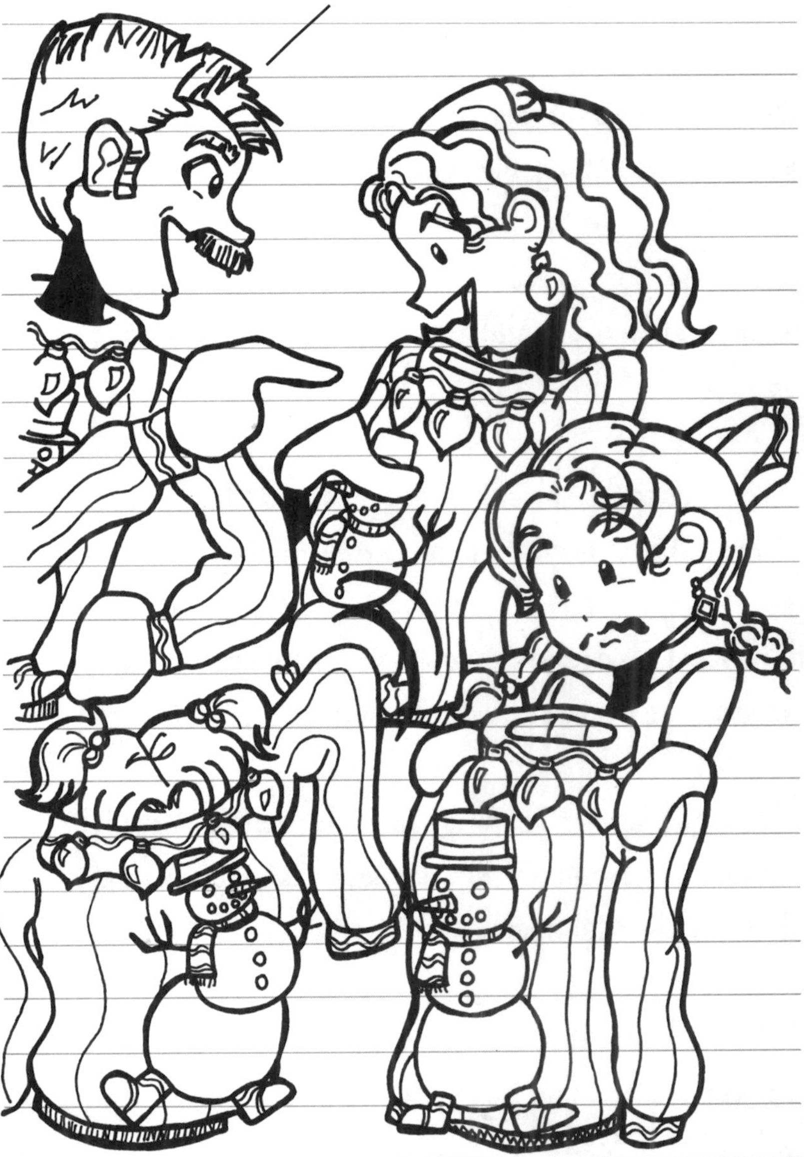

Dad set up his camera, and we gathered in front of our Christmas tree.

Then he set the timer and quickly took his place next to Mom.

"Okay! Everyone say 'Cheese!'" he said.

However, right before the flash went off, Brianna must have decided she wanted a little snack or something.

Because suddenly she turned and yanked at a candy cane hooked on a tree branch.

OMG! I couldn't believe the whole tree fell over.

It was totally a Maxwell family moment.

I laughed so hard my ribs hurt.

I have to admit, this family portrait is now my favorite.

Unfortunately, Mom decided we looked SO ADORABLE in our snowman sweaters, she wants us all to wear them to dinner at my aunt Mabel's house tomorrow.

I was like, JUST GREAT ☹!! My aunt Mabel is NOT exactly my favorite relative.

It was going to be like having dinner with AUNTY SCROOGE!

THIS is the woman who STILL insists that I sit at the dreaded KIDDIE TABLE!

Any holiday spirit I had, leaked right out of me.

Just thinking about the kiddie table made me so anxious I thought I was going to have a complete meltdown.

To survive this ordeal, I was going to need nothing short of a Christmas miracle!

!!

Today is Christmas Day!

Brianna woke us up by banging on our bedroom doors and screaming hysterically.

Just like she does every year.

And it's always the EXACT same story. . . .

"Wake up, everybody! Wake up! Me and Miss Penelope just saw Santa and his reindeer leaving. They flew right off our roof and over Mrs. Wallabanger's house. Wake up! It's an emergency!"

Then we all rush downstairs in our pajamas to see

what Santa has left and open our presents together.

As usual, Brianna got a ton of stuff. . . .

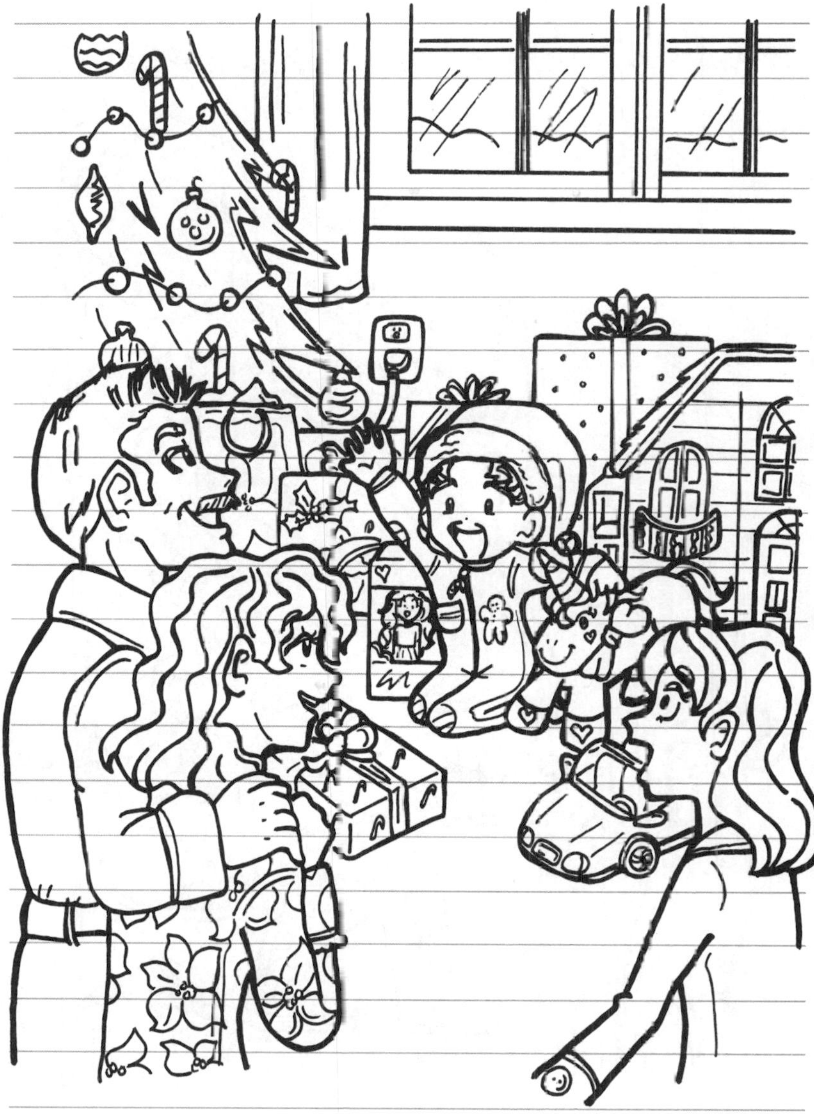

Mom and Dad LOVED the scrapbook that Brianna and I made (which included that hilarious photo of our Christmas tree falling over). . . .

MOM & DAD, LOVING THEIR SCRAPBOOK

But the very BEST present was . . .

MY BRAND-NEW CELL PHONE!!

Soon it was time to go to my aunt Mabel's for our holiday dinner. Dad says his oldest sister is just old-fashioned and kind of strict. But I think "strict" is just a nicer word for "MEAN."

Mom says Aunt Mabel acts like that because she thinks kids should be seen and not heard.

Personally, I think Aunt Mabel just HATES kids because she has nine of them.

OMG!! If I gave birth NINE whole times, I wouldn't want to SEE them or HEAR them! I'm just sayin'.

But get this! I'm fourteen years old. And that EVIL woman STILL made me sit at the KIDDIE TABLE!

The adults sat in the dining room at a hand-carved antique table with Queen Anne chairs, fancy porcelain china, crystal glasses, and gold-plated silverware.

The kiddie table was a wobbly, child-size card table covered with a worn-out bedsheet.

We got paper plates, plastic forks, and those teeny-tiny paper cups (you know, the ones you use in your bathroom when you brush your teeth).

And sitting at the kiddie table while wearing my snowman sweater meant I was twice as humiliated.

ME, SITTING AT THE KIDDIE TABLE

The whole thing was a very traumatic experience.

Thank goodness the food was delicious, or it would have been a totally worthless visit.

My aunt Mabel is as mean as a pit bull, but she's an excellent cook.

Anyway, I was really happy when we finally made it back home, because I got to play around with my new cell phone.

I CANNOT believe all the cool stuff it has, like Internet, texting, e-mail, instant messaging, games, camera, homework help, automatic pizza delivery, and a teen peer counseling hotline.

OMG! If cell phones paid an ALLOWANCE, parents would be OBSOLETE!

Brianna went NUTS because my phone came with the game Princess Sugar Plum Saves Baby Unicorn Island. I let her play it for an hour right before bedtime, and now she's, like, totally addicted.

My new phone is going to save me a ton of money.

Now whenever I need to bribe Brianna to do

something, I simply pay her with Princess Sugar Plum game minutes instead of cash.

It took me a while to figure it out, but I took a picture of me with my phone and sent it to Chloe, Zoey, and Brandon.

They are going to be supershocked and surprised when they receive it.

Overall, my Christmas was pretty good.

It started snowing outside and actually looked like a winter wonderland.

Then Dad lit the fireplace and we all roasted

marshmallows together. Again! Only this time Dad's pants didn't catch on fire.

I have to admit . . . Once you get used to them, having a family to hang out with can be kind of nice.

I wonder how Brandon's Christmas is going?

It's really admirable that he helps out his grandparents by volunteering at Fuzzy Friends. I throw a hissy fit when I have to clean my room and put dishes in the dishwasher.

I'm SUCH a spoiled BRAT! And I don't really appreciate the blessings I have, like my family.

It's just mind-boggling how he's lost pretty much everything, yet he continues to have so much to GIVE!

Now, THAT'S truly a CHRISTMAS MIRACLE!

☺!!

THURSDAY, DECEMBER 26

Today was our first practice session with Victoria Steel, the *Holiday on Ice* show director and Olympic gold medalist figure skater.

Everyone participating in the show received a welcome letter and a list of rules:

VICTORIA STEEL'S SHOW RULES

1. NO AUTOGRAPHS
2. NO GUM CHEWING
3. NO UGLY SKATING OUTFITS
4. NO HAIRY LEGS

All skaters are to be prompt, courteous, and prepared.

Unsportsmanlike behavior will not be tolerated, and any violation will result in automatic dismissal from the *Holiday on Ice* show.

GOOD LUCK!
VICTORIA STEEL

All we have to do now is survive three days of practice with Victoria.

My biggest fear is that she's going to kick me out of the show like she did to that poor girl last year. Chloe insisted it was probably just a rumor, but I wasn't taking any chances. After scrounging around in our garage, I found the perfect costume for our first practice.

I was a nervous wreck when Mom dropped me off for practice at the ice arena.

All I could think of was Brandon having to start a new school in January without any friends.

Since I didn't want anyone to see my costume, I avoided the crowded locker room and got dressed in a small bathroom on the far side of the arena instead.

I stared at my reflection in the mirror and smiled. I knew I looked ridiculous.

But if my plan worked, at least I'd make it through the first practice.

By the time I made my way back to the rink, most of the skaters were already on the ice practicing, including Chloe and Zoey.

I was amazed at how graceful they were, and I couldn't help but feel proud of them.

Near the main entrance, a large crowd surrounded Victoria. She was pretty and looked surprisingly similar to the girl on the cover of *The Ice Princess*.

Fans took pictures of her with their cell phones and waited in line for an autograph.

And like a pop star, she traveled with her own entourage and security detail.

As Victoria rushed past me she took off her sunglasses and let out an irritated sigh.

"Let's get this over with! I just hope this group

is better than last year's! Can someone get me a water? I'm about to die of thirst!"

Her staffers scrambled in different directions, and within thirty seconds two assistants and two security guys offered her bottled waters.

"OMG! You expect me to drink water from a PLASTIC bottle?" she shrieked.

One thing was quite obvious. The woman was a spoiled diva!

The assistant director asked all the skaters to take a seat in the first two rows.

He then introduced Victoria as the skaters cheered excitedly.

In spite of her meltdown over the bottled water situation, she immediately plastered a fake smile on her face.

"So! Who'd like to impress me first?" she asked,

eyeing the list of names on her clipboard. "Let's start with a group. How about . . ."

My heart skipped a beat.

Please don't call us! Please don't call us! Please don't call us! I chanted inside my head.

". . . Chloe, Zoey, and Nikki. Front and center!"

Chloe and Zoey quickly scrambled onto the ice.

"Why do I only see two of you, instead of three?" Victoria asked with a highly annoyed glare.

"Um . . . Nikki should be here. Somewhere!" Zoey answered, and glanced nervously at Chloe.

"Here I am," I said as I carefully made my way onto the ice.

Chloe and Zoey took one look at me, gasped, and shrieked . . .

NIKKI, WHAT HAPPENED?!!

That's when I realized my fake cast made from toilet paper and white duct tape actually looked pretty real. Especially with Dad's old crutches from that time he went bungee jumping.

"Don't worry. It's not as bad as it looks," I answered.

"OMG! Is it broken?" Chloe asked.

"You poor thing!" Zoey exclaimed.

"I'm FINE! REALLY!" I said, and kind of winked. Chloe and Zoey looked at me and then at each other. I think they got the hint.

"So, you're Nikki?" Victoria asked, staring me down. "I'm really sorry about your accident, but I have a show to run here. You three are just going to have to participate next year. Sorry, girls!"

"NO! PLEASE! Actually, it's just a little sprain. My doctor assured me I'd be fine by—by, um . . . tomorrow," I stammered.

That's when Victoria suddenly narrowed her eyes at my cast and stared at me suspiciously. "So, your doctor uses DUCT TAPE?!" Then she put her hands on her hips and yelled . . .

I could NOT believe that crazy lady actually called
security on me like that. She's NUTZ!!

"Chloe and Zoey, get into position—now! I want
to see this routine!" she shouted. "But I'm warning

you! If the THREE of you are NOT ready to skate tomorrow, you'll be disqualified! Understood?"

We nodded.

As I hurried off the ice, I gave Chloe and Zoey a thumbs-up, and they smiled at me nervously. As long as I wasn't out there messing things up, they were going to do fine.

And I was right. They both skated flawlessly, and Victoria was both surprised and impressed.

I decided not to hang around for the rest of the practice session. I'd had quite enough of Victoria Steel for one day, and I was sure the feeling was mutual.

I hobbled back to the bathroom, anxious to ditch the uncomfortable crutches and itchy cast. I was about to call my mom to pick me up, when an uninvited guest barged into the bathroom.

It was MACKENZIE!! And boy, was she ticked!

YOU'RE A PATHETIC LITTLE PHONY!

I was going to bat my eyes all innocentlike and completely DENY the whole fake-cast thing.

265

But then I realized my crutches were leaning against the wall and I was standing there perfectly fine on my "injured" ankle.

OOPS!!

Phony or not, MY personal health issues were none of MacKenzie's business.

"You're calling ME a phony?" I huffed. "You're wearing SO many hair extensions and SO much lip gloss, the fire marshal has declared you a fire hazard due to a high risk of spontaneous combustion!"

OMG! MacKenzie was so angry I thought her head was going to explode.

She stared at me with her beady little eyes and hissed, "I've already warned Victoria about you. Make one more wrong step and she'll throw you out of this show faster than a ten-day-old moldy pizza."

Then she turned and sashayed away.

I hate it when MacKenzie sashays!

I could NOT believe she was trying to boss me around like that. I mean, just WHO does she think she is?! The ICE-SKATING POLICE?!

Anyway, the good news is that I actually survived the first *Holiday on Ice* practice session with Victoria the Dragon Lady.

ONE down and TWO more to go.

☺!!

After Victoria threatened us yesterday, I didn't dare show up with that fake cast again.

I had tossed and turned most of the night, trying to come up with another plan.

But the sad truth was that it was pretty much over for me.

As soon as Victoria took one look at me ~~skating~~ scooting around on the ice, she was going to kick Chloe, Zoey, and me right out of her show.

And it didn't help that MacKenzie was probably telling her awful stuff about me. Like that I stole Fuzzy Friends and my broken leg was fake.

Well, okay! So maybe the broken leg thing WAS fake. But still! It was none of that girl's business.

When Victoria started screaming at the music guy, the lights guy, and the wardrobe guy (OMG! That crazy lady did A LOT of SCREAMING), I decided to sneak away and hide out up in the stands for a few minutes.

Then I could have my massive panic attack in private.

I was deep in thought, pondering my hopeless situation, when a very familiar voice startled me.

"So, what does it feel like to be an Ice Princess?"

"BRANDON! What are you doing here?" I gasped.

"I came to thank you for making me that awesome scrapbook! And to cheer on Team Fuzzy Friends!"

This guy was too nice to be real! The possibility that he might move away was just . . . too depressing!

Suddenly I was overcome with emotion. I had to bite my lip to keep from bursting into tears.

Brandon's warm smile slowly vanished, and he just stared at me in silence.

"Nikki! Are you okay? What's wrong . . . ?"

"I'm sorry, Brandon! But I don't know if I'm going to be able to earn that money to help Fuzzy Friends. I'm just . . . SO sorry! I really am!"

"What do you mean? No one expects you to be a pro. Just being in the show is enough."

"NO! It's NOT. I have to be able to SKATE in the show. And I CAN'T! But I didn't know that at the time I volunteered to help. Honest!"

"Come on, Nikki! You CAN'T be that bad!"

"Brandon, listen to me. I'm THAT bad! No! Actually, I'm WORSE! I seriously expect to get kicked out of the show after we skate today."

Brandon blinked his eyes in disbelief.

"Victoria requires that skaters be prepared to skate, and I'm NOT! I can barely stand on the ice, let alone skate on it!"

We just sat there in silence as the sheer hopelessness of my situation sank in

If I DIDN'T skate, Fuzzy Friends would close and Brandon would be moving!

And if I DID skate, Fuzzy Friends would close and Brandon would be moving!

It was a LOSE-LOSE situation.

"I'm sorry, Nikki. I wish there was something I could do . . . ," Brandon muttered as he stared down at Victoria, who was now screaming at the Zamboni guy.

My heart started to pound when she announced over the speaker system that Chloe, Zoey, and I were up next.

Brandon gave me a weak smile.

"Break a leg! Actually, try NOT to break a leg! Sorry."

"Thanks!" I said, smiling at his little joke.

Brandon didn't know it, but I'd ALREADY tried using that "broken leg" thing on Victoria.

Been there, done that!

When I got down to the rink, I could tell Chloe and Zoey were supernervous too, but they were trying their best not to show it.

"Okay, Team Fuzzy! Group hug!" Chloe said, and did her jazz hands to try to lighten the mood.

Somehow I made it onto the ice and got into position without falling.

And just as our music began, I saw Brandon approach Victoria with his camera and tap her on her shoulder.

When she turned around, he introduced himself and pointed to his camera.

Apparently, Victoria was immediately charmed by his professionalism, good manners, and smile.

Which was a really good thing, because our skating routine was NOT going so well. . . .

Coincidentally (or not), Brandon's impromptu photo shoot lasted until the final note of our music.

And when Victoria FINALLY turned around . . .

We plastered big smiles on our faces and struck a superFIERCE pose. Like we were the top three finalists on *America's Next Top Model* or something.

No one ever would have guessed I had just fallen four times during our three-minute routine.

OMG! I'd spent so much time sliding around on my BUTT, it had frostbite.

Victoria just stared at us with this strange look on her face as we held our breath.

"Great job, girls!!" she finally said, and turned to her assistant. "WHERE is my cappuccino? Am I supposed to run this show AND do YOUR job?!"

Brandon gave me a huge smile and winked.

I wanted to MELT into a puddle right there on the ice.

Of course, when I walked past MacKenzie, she glared at me and held her nose.

But I already knew I completely STANK as a skater.

She didn't have to remind me.

Anyway, I CANNOT believe we're STILL in the show.

Brandon is such a SWEETHEART!! I could not believe he helped us out like that.

TWO practice sessions DOWN.

And ONE to go!

WOO-HOO!!

☺!!

BRIANNA AND I GO SLEDDING
(A TERRIFYING EXPERIENCE)

BRIANNA, ARE YOU SURE ABOUT
DEAD MAN'S DROP? IT MIGHT BE KINDA
SCARY FOR A LITTLE KID LIKE YOU!

THERE IT IS!

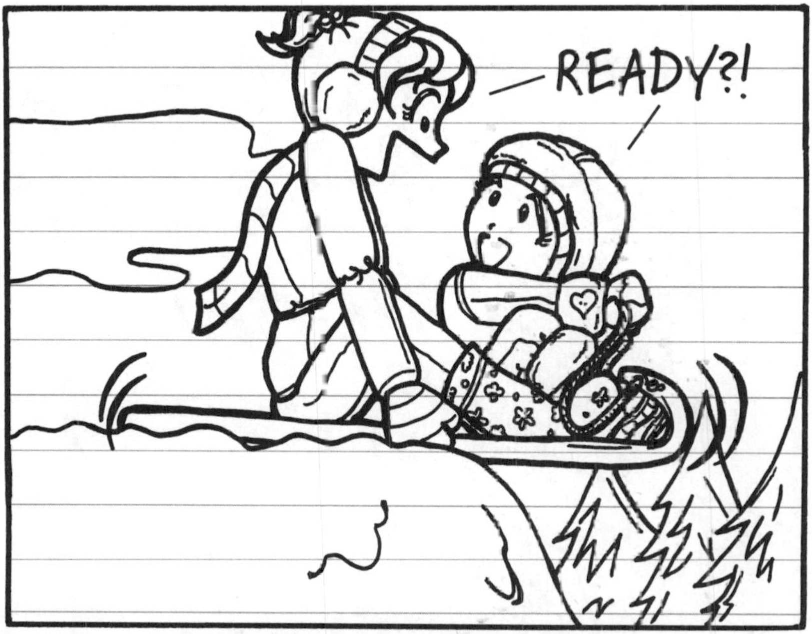
READY?!

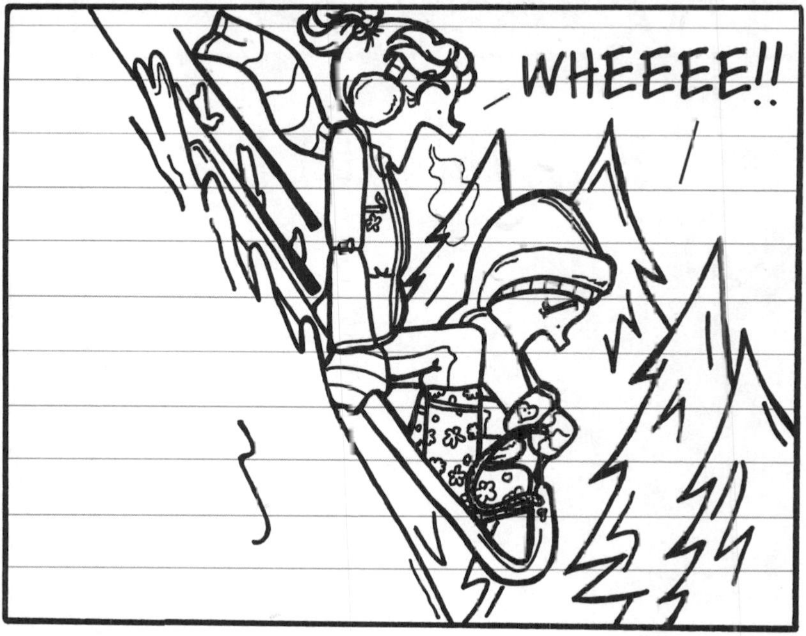
WHEEEEE!!

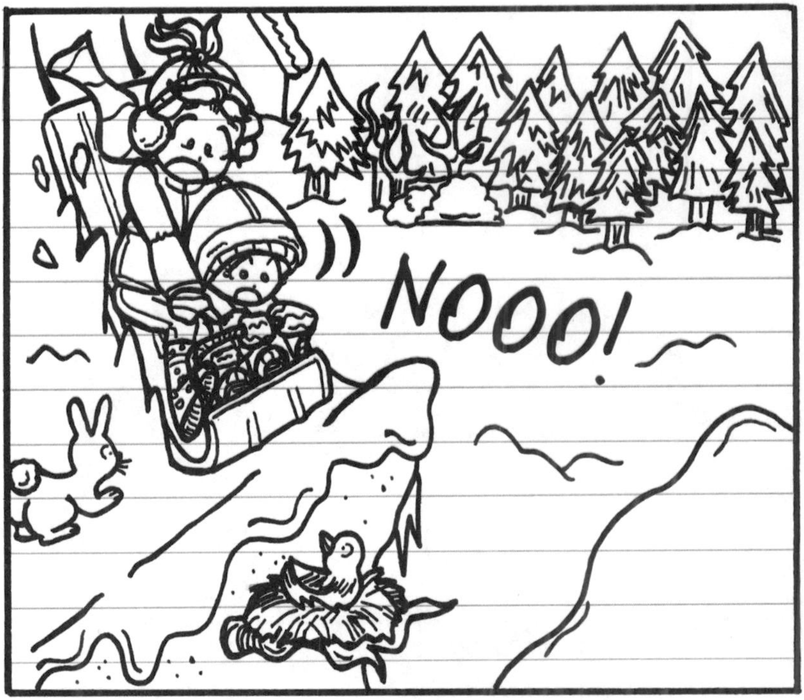
NOOO!

TO BE CONTINUED . . . !!

☹!!

SUNDAY, DECEMBER 29

BRIANNA AND I GO SLEDDING
(A TERRIFYING EXPERIENCE)
CONTINUED . . .

When we last saw our heroes, Brianna and Nikki, they were speeding down a towering cliff, about to plummet to their deaths. But just when it seemed like they were DOOMED . . .

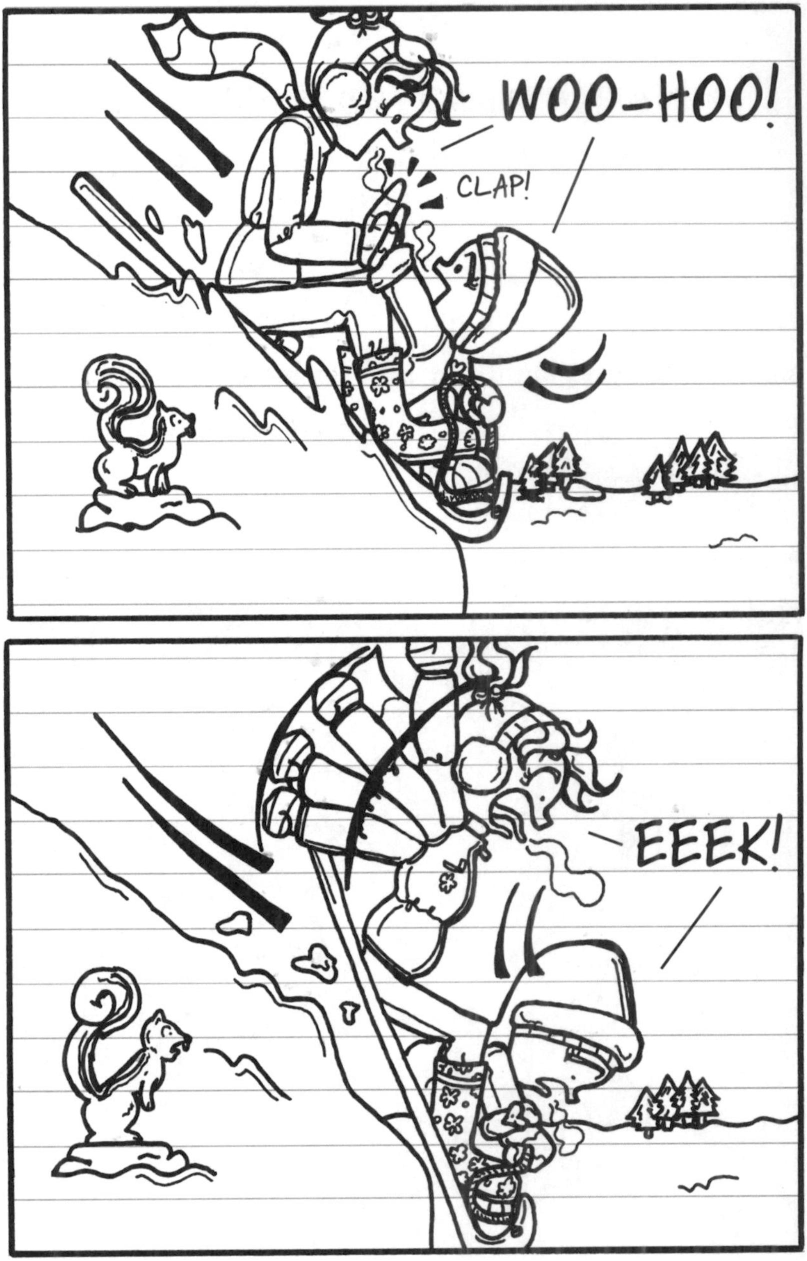
WOO-HOO!
CLAP!
EEEK!

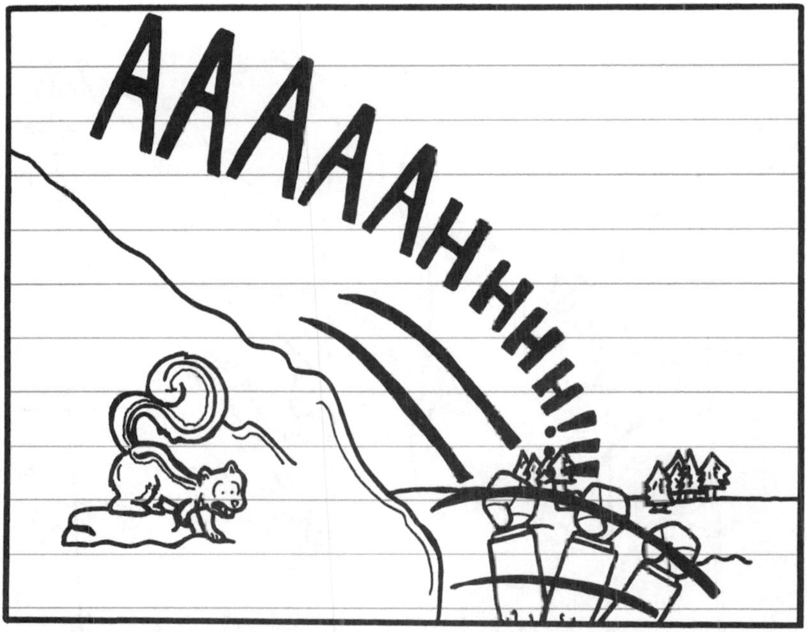
AAAAAAHHHHH!!!!

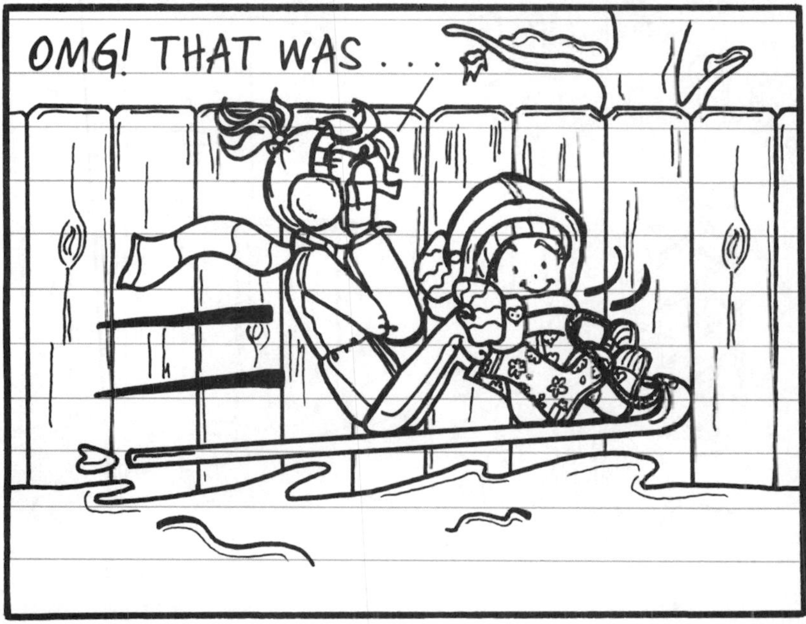
OMG! THAT WAS . . . .

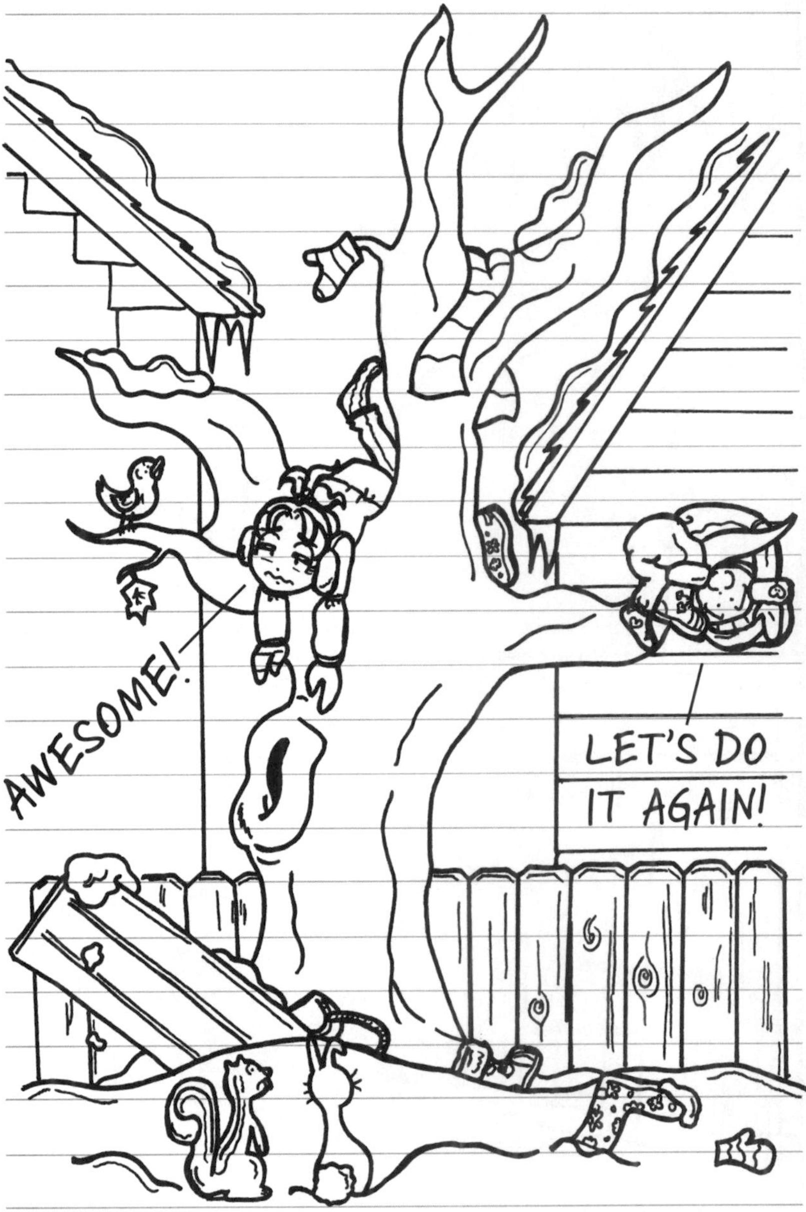
AWESOME!
LET'S DO IT AGAIN!
THE END

My parents' priorities are totally screwed up.

Mom had to rush off to visit a friend who'd just had a baby.

And Dad had an emergency call from some rich lady whose fancy dinner party had been crashed by some unexpected guests. About two thousand ants!

Guess WHO got stuck babysitting Brianna?

ME! That's who!

Even though that meant I had to bring her with me to an EXTREMELY important practice session at the ice-skating arena that involved $3,000 and possibly LIFE and DEATH!

A new BABY is born somewhere in the world every seven seconds and ANTS will still be around even after a nuclear war.

HOW in the world was what THEY were doing MORE important than what I was doing?!

"Nikki, just call me on my cell when you're done with practice," Mom said as she pulled up in front of the arena. "And, Brianna, you be a good girl and mind your sister, okay?"

"Okay, Mommy!" Brianna beamed like a little angel.

Then she turned and stuck her tongue out at me.

"Nikki, can I play Princess Sugar Plum on your phone?" Brianna asked as we entered the building.

It was the fifth time she had asked me that today.

"No, Brianna, you're here to watch the ice skaters."

Chloe and Zoey were already on the ice practicing. But when they saw Brianna, they rushed over and gave her a big hug.

Brianna was fascinated by the skaters and sat

quietly and watched. I could hardly believe she was behaving so well.

About twenty-five minutes later Victoria called our names.

"We're up!" Zoey said with a nervous smile. "Are you ready, Nikki?"

I took a deep breath and stepped forward to meet my destiny. I was so nervous, I thought I was going to lose my Egg McMuffin.

I'd managed to get through the first two practices without Victoria tossing me out.

But short of a major miracle, I thought it was finally the end of the line for me.

Once she actually saw me skate, or more correctly, TRY to skate, I was SO out of the show.

"Final call!" Victoria said sharply. "Chloe, Zoey, and Nikki!"

As we hustled onto the ice, Victoria watched us like a hawk. I tried my hardest NOT to fall.

We were just about to get into our starting positions when suddenly there was a major disruption from the stands. . . .

HEY, YOU GUYS, I WANNA SLIDE ON THE ICE TOO!

I skated over, grabbed Brianna's hand, and escorted her back to her seat!

"Brianna! Are you trying to get us kicked out of the show?" I hissed. "Sit right there and DON'T! MOVE!"

She gave me her saddest puppy-dog eyes. "But, Nikki! I want to slide on the ice with you, Chloe, and Zoey!"

Victoria looked like she was going to blow a gasket. But since there was a camera crew nearby, she just stretched her lips into a cold, mannequinlike smile and batted her eyes really fast.

As I turned to go back on the ice, a guy in a blue uniform stopped me.

"Excuse me, but I have a flower delivery for a Victoria Steel. It's from the mayor's office. I was told to leave them at the front desk, but it's closed. Do you know who she is?"

"Sure, she's right over there," I said, pointing.

Victoria appeared to be doing an impromptu live interview with a TV reporter.

"Well, I don't want to interrupt her. But I'm running behind schedule on my deliveries. Could you do me a favor and see to it that she gets these?"

"No problem!" I said.

He placed a beautiful bouquet of two dozen pink roses on the seat next to Brianna.

"Oooh! Those are really PRETTY!" Brianna squealed. "Are they yours?"

"No, they're for that lady over there!" I said, pointing to Victoria. "I have to give them to her."

"Nikki, can I give them to her?" Brianna asked excitedly.

"Don't even think about it! Stay in your seat!"

That's when I got the most brilliant idea!

"Actually, Brianna, it would be a BIG help if you'd take these flowers over to Victoria!" I said happily.

"Goody gumdrops!" she cheered.

"But I need you to be really careful with them. I'm going to wave at you when it's time. Okay?"

"Okay. Can I smell them too? I bet they smell like cotton candy! Or bubble gum!"

I took my place on the ice next to Chloe and Zoey, but I was so nervous, I couldn't think straight.

Just as the music was about to start, I waved at Brianna to signal her to take the flowers to Victoria.

Only Brianna just smiled and waved back at me.

I waved at her again and this time pointed at the flowers. But Brianna just waved and pointed at the flowers too.

JUST GREAT ☹!!

As music blared over the speakers, Chloe and Zoey moved gracefully over the ice.

But I stood there in my pose, waving my arms in slow motion and wishing I could skate over and strangle Brianna.

After what seemed like FOREVER, Brianna finally got a clue. She snatched up the bouquet of roses and trudged off toward Victoria.

Brianna tugged on Victoria's coat, and when the woman turned around, a wide smile spread across her face.

"Psst!" Chloe whispered. "Nikki! SKATE!"

I took off gliding across the ice, immediately lost my balance, and fell to my knees.

Brianna smiled and handed Victoria the bouquet of flowers.

"For me?" She gushed like she had just been
awarded another gold medal or something.

Then I tripped over Chloe's foot, collided with
Zoey, and slid across the ice on my butt. It was . . .
SURREAL!

Totally flattered by Brianna's borrowed gift, Victoria grabbed a pen and paper and gave Brianna her autograph.

And because Brianna was equally as vain as the celebrity skater, she insisted on giving Victoria HER autograph too.

Then Brianna gave Victoria a big hug.

Of course the TV cameras captured every second.

It seemed like all that gushing, hugging, and smiling went on, like, FOREVER. Or at least, long enough for us to finish our routine.

Once again we struck a FIERCE ending pose and waited breathlessly for the verdict.

When Victoria finally turned around and faced us, she was practically glowing.

Hugging her bouquet in one arm and Brianna in the other, she smiled and said . . .

As Chloe, Zoey, and I blinked in astonishment,
Brianna cheered for us. Very loudly.

But, hey! Who were WE to disagree with the great and wonderful Victoria Steel?

And her, um . . . trusty sidekick, Brianna!

So right now I'm NOT that mad at Mom and Dad about this whole babysitting thing.

The amazing thing is that I actually SURVIVED THREE whole practice sessions with THE Victoria Steel, BANSHEE DIVA of the figure skating world!

Now if I could just make it through our entire performance tomorrow, Fuzzy Friends Animal Rescue Center will be saved and Brandon won't have to move away.

I'm so NOT looking forward to publicly humiliating myself by tripping, slipping, and stumbling my way through our routine tomorrow.

But I'm willing to do whatever I have to do.

And I'm STILL really worried that MacKenzie is

going to pull some kind of stunt at the last minute to get us kicked out of the show.

Even though she hasn't said anything to me since our little blow-up ir the bathroom a few days ago, every time I see her, she just stares at me the way a very hungry snake looks at a mouse.

That girl is RUTHLESS.

She'll do just about anything to anybody to get whatever she wants.

I will be SO relieved when the *Holiday on Ice* show is finally OVER!

!!

OMG! OMG! OMG! I cannot believe what just happened! I guess I should just start at the beginning. . . .

The _Holiday on Ice_ show is well-known for its fabulous costumes. And this year Victoria Steel borrowed them from the private collection of a famous, award-winning Broadway producer.

At 9:00 a.m., everyone met with the wardrobe manager for a final fitting and costume check.

Chloe, Zoey, and I were skating to the classical holiday piece "Dance of the Sugar Plum Fairy" from _The Nutcracker._

That was because Chloe and Zoey were dying to wear a superglitzy costume like the heroine in _The Ice Princess._

Well, my BFFs got their wish! The fairy costumes Victoria selected for us were AMAZING!

I almost fell over in shock when MacKenzie actually complimented us.

She said she loved our gorgeous costumes and they were her very favorites.

After our fitting was over, we spent the morning at a swanky spa getting manicures and pedicures. Then we visited a salon for hair and makeup.

Talk about GLAM! We were ready for the cover of *Girls' Life* magazine!

After we grabbed a quick lunch, it was almost 2:00 p.m. and time to head back to the arena to get dressed for the 4:00 p.m. show.

Even though I was a nervous wreck about skating in front of a thousand people, my only goal was to finish that routine. Even if it killed me.

Then Fuzzy Friends would be awarded the money and Brandon could stay at WCD ☺!

But unfortunately, what started off as a great day was quickly ruined when we realized . . .

OUR SUGAR PLUM FAIRY COSTUMES WERE
MISSING!! AND IN THEIR PLACE WERE . . .

CLOWN COSTUMES?!

When we reported the situation to the wardrobe manager, she and her staff spent thirty minutes searching for our fairy costumes.

But they were nowhere to be found.

I had a sneaking suspicion MacKenzie had something to do with the disappearance.

She had this nasty little smirk on her face and was snickering at our new costumes. But I had no proof whatsoever.

Apparently, Victoria had ordered the clowns and three other costumes but had decided not to use them.

All the extra costumes had been picked up by a delivery service at noon to be transported back to New York City. But SOMEHOW our costumes and the clown ones had gotten switched.

This meant our beautiful Sugar Plum Fairy costumes were already halfway back to New York City by now.

We were devastated! Chloe and Zoey were so upset
they started to cry.

"Come on, guys!" I said. "Don't be upset. We can
STILL do this!"

"But I was really looking forward to being an Ice
Princess!" Chloe whimpered.

"Me too!" Zoey sniffed

"But don't you see? This is about more than just
looking glamorous. We're doing this for Fuzzy Friends.

Remember?!" I said, trying to give them a pep talk.

"And, yes, I know!" I continued. "These clown costumes are freakishly ugly, and we'll probably look scary and a little insane. And the kids at school will make fun of us for the rest of the year, and we'll probably be an embarrassment to our parents. But look at the bright side . . ."

Chloe and Zoey looked at me expectantly. "What's the bright side?" they both asked.

"Well, um . . . actually. It's . . . um. Okay! So maybe there ISN'T a BRIGHT side! But a lot of nice people and cute little fuzzy animals are depending on us! Just ask yourself, what would Crystal Coldstone, the Ice Princess, do?"

Suddenly Chloe wiped her tears and placed her hands on her hips. "Well, Crystal would kick butt and send those Vambies packing! That's what she'd do!"

"And she'd wear a freakishly ugly clown costume if it meant saving humankind!" Zoey added.

Then Zoey lowered her voice to almost a whisper. "The art of the clown is more profound than we think. . . . It is the COMIC mirror of tragedy, and the TRAGIC mirror of comedy—André Suarès."

FINALLY! I seemed to be getting through to my BFFs.

"Come on, girlfriends!" I said. "LET'S DO THIS THING!!"

That's when we did a group hug!

It was a little weird going from glamorous Sugar Plum Fairies to a pathetic clown posse, but as we got dressed we tried to keep a positive attitude.

In spite of the new costumes, we decided to keep our original music and skating routine.

Especially since we'd been practicing it for the past two weeks.

Soon Mom and Brianna came back to the dressing room to wish us luck. When Brianna saw our new clown costumes, she got really excited.

"Hey, guess what? When I grow up, I'm going to slide on the ice and be a scary, stupid-looking clown too, just like you guys!" she gushed.

I think that was a compliment, but I'm not sure.

Brianna picked up my cell phone from the dressing room table, and her eyes lit up.

NIKKI, CAN I PLAY THE PRINCESS SUGAR PLUM GAME ON YOUR CELL WHILE YOU, CHLOE, AND ZOEY ARE SLIDING ON THE ICE?

"No, Brianna. I told you NEVER to touch my phone unless I say you can. Remember?"

"Pretty please!" Brianna whined. "I promise I won't break it." Then she shoved my phone behind her back so I couldn't reach it.

"MOM!" I whined even louder than Brianna.

"Brianna Maxwell!" Mom scolded. "You know the rule. Your sister's cell phone is off-limits unless she gives you permission. Now hand it over!"

Brianna gave Mom her saddest puppy-dog eyes and then pouted like a two-year-old. But she finally surrendered my phone, and I snatched it from her.

"Me and Miss Penelope think you're a MEANIE!" Brianna said, sticking her tongue out at me.

"Fine. Then YOU and MISS PENELOPE can NEVER, EVER play the Princess Sugar Plum game on MY phone for the rest of your LIVES! So THERE!"

Then I stuck my tongue out at both of them.

"Okay, girls! That's enough!" Mom scolded Brianna and me.

I placed my phone back on my dressing table.

But when I saw Brianna watching me like a hawk, I stuck it inside that cute little pocket on my purse and stuffed my purse in my backpack with the rest of my clothes.

Just as Mom and Brianna were leaving, the assistant stage manager announced that the show would be starting in forty-five minutes. All of us skaters had to check in with the stage manager across the hall.

"I gotta use the bathroom!" Brianna whined really loudly. "NOW!"

She was SUCH an embarrassment!

Chloe showed Brianna and Mom the door to the bathroom in our dressing room.

Then we rushed off to check in.

When we came back to our dressing room to grab our skates and start warm-ups, we saw a note posted on the door.

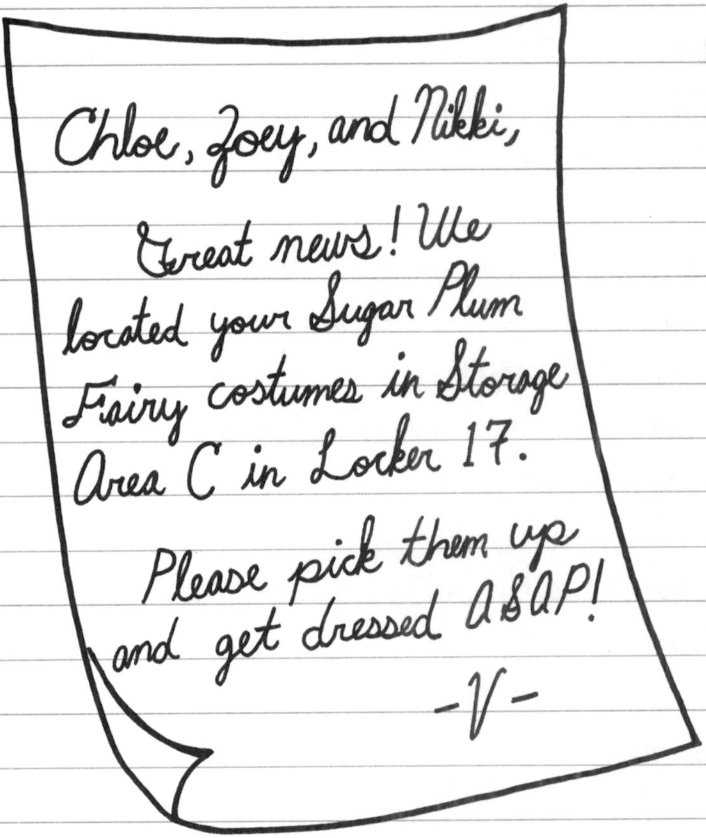
Chloe, Zoey, and Nikki,
Great news! We located your Sugar Plum Fairy costumes in Storage Area C in Locker 17.
Please pick them up and get dressed ASAP!
-V-

The wardrobe manager had found our costumes! We were so happy, we did a group hug and started screaming.

"OMG! They finally found them!" I screamed.

"Just in time!" Zoey screamed.

"We're going to be Ice Princesses after all!" Chloe screamed.

"LET'S GO!" I yelled as we took off running down the hall. "We only have thirty minutes before the show starts!"

Suddenly Chloe stopped.

"Wait! I'm going to grab my cell phone so we can call our moms and let them know they found our Sugar Plum Fairy costumes. Plus, we need to wash off the clown makeup and put on the fairy makeup, and we're going to need their help!"

"Great idea!" Zoey and I exclaimed.

Storage Area C was on the other side of the arena, near the hockey player locker rooms. All team practices had been canceled due to the ice show, so the halls were dark, shadowy, and strangely quiet.

"Is it me, or is this place kind of creepy?" Zoey said nervously.

"We're just going to grab our costumes and get out of here," Chloe assured her.

"Okay. Storage locker fourteen, fifteen, sixteen," I counted out loud, "and seventeen! Here it is, guys!"

The closet was closed by a simple latch on the outside.

We opened it and peered in. It was even darker inside.

"Don't be skurd!" I teased. "It's just a walk-in storage closet," I said as we all stepped inside.

"Is there a light in here?" Zoey asked.

"Hey! Let's use my cell phone," Chloe suggested. "It lights up!"

She held it up high in the center of the storage area, and it cast an eerie green glow.

"Thanks, that's a lot better," I said. "Okay, I see hockey sticks, pucks, and ice skates. But no Sugar Plum Fairy costu—"

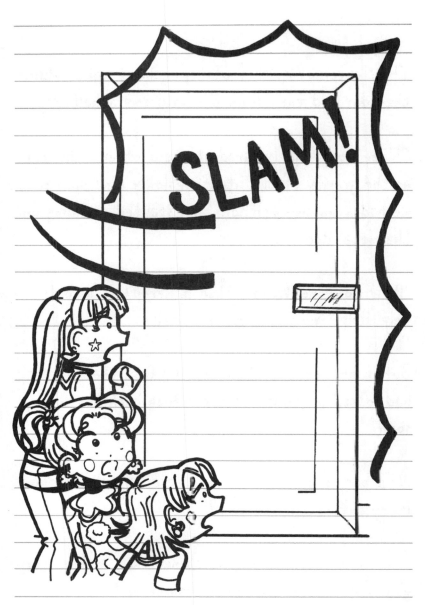

The huge metal door suddenly slammed shut. Then I
heard the outside latch slide into place.

KLA-CHUNK!

The clatter of quick footsteps echoed right outside the door and then down the long, empty hallway.

Chloe, Zoey, and I stared at one another in horror as the gravity of our situation slowly sank in. Then we had a massive meltdown and started pounding on the metal door like crazy.

"Help! Someone! We're locked in here! Let us out! Help! Help!" we screamed frantically.

But it became quite clear pretty fast that whoever had locked us inside was not coming back anytime soon.

We'd been set up. There were never any Sugar Plum Fairy costumes in locker 17.

And all we could do was watch nervously as the green glow from Chloe's phone got dimmer and dimmer.

"Sorry, guys. I think I forgot to charge my phone.

But I think I can make three or four calls before it goes completely dead. Any suggestions?"

For about thirty seconds it was so quiet in the room you could hear a pin drop.

"Let's try calling our moms first," Zoey offered.

"Good idea!" Chloe and I agreed.

But it wasn't. All three of their phones went straight to voice mail. Which meant they were probably already turned off so as not to ring during the show.

Still, we each left a detailed voice message.

The GOOD news was that at the very worst, our moms would retrieve our messages AFTER the ice show was over and come looking for us.

So it was just a matter of time before we got rescued.

But the BAD news was that we were going to be

stuck in the storage locker for two very long, dark, spooky hours until they showed up.

"One call left. If we're lucky!" Chloe announced, staring at her phone.

"Well, I think we should call 911!" Zoey said.

"True, but by the time they got us out of here we'd still miss our performance," Chloe reasoned.

"Yeah, the show starts in fifteen minutes," I said, looking at my watch.

"You're right," Zoey conceded. "And it's going to be pretty darn embarrassing when they show up with three police cars, two fire trucks, and an ambulance just to unlatch a storage room door. We'll never live it down."

"They'll probably STILL be laughing at us at our high school graduation," Chloe mused. "I'd rather just wait for our moms to get here after the show."

I could NOT believe I had come this far only to be stuck in a storage unit inside the ice arena with the show starting in twelve minutes.

I got a huge lump in my throat thinking about Brandon. Now he was going to have to leave his home and friends at WCD and start over again.

I felt terrible for him. But I was powerless. Signing up for this stupid show was a HUGE mistake.

If only I'd just let MacKenzie skate for Fuzzy Friends like she'd wanted. Then Brandon's life would not have to be turned upside down again. My heart hurt just thinking about the stuff he'd been through.

He had lost his parents, and I totally took mine for granted.

Hot tears began to sting my eyes, but I blinked them back. I heard Chloe and Zoey starting to sniffle too.

Brandon was going to leave just when we were
starting to get to know each other.

Brianna was such a BRAT to him, but he still gave her
that cute thank-you note from the puppies and—

That's when a little lightbulb went on in my brain.

BRIANNA THE BRAT?!

YES! My nutty little sister, who I could always count on to be a total PAIN in the butt.

"Chloe! I've got an idea! Dial my cell phone number! Quick! Before your phone dies!"

"What? But why?" Chloe asked. "Didn't you leave it in the dressing room? Everyone was supposed to be dressed and cleared out of there thirty minutes ago."

"I know! Just call! PLEASE! We're running out of time! The show starts in ten minutes!"

Chloe and Zoey stared at me like I was nuts.

Finally Chloe shrugged, called my cell phone, and put it on speaker so we all could hear.

It rang once. Twice. Then three times.

I had set it up so that it would go to voice mail on the fifth ring.

"Please answer! Please answer!" I pleaded aloud.

It rang a fourth time. Then . . .

"Hello! Who is this?" said a small, squeaky voice.

OMG! BRIANNA! You have my cell phone?! Thank goodness!

Chloe and Zoey started screaming excitedly too.

"Sorry, but this isn't me," Brianna continued. "I'm not home right now because I'm waiting for Nikki to skate. Please leave a message. Good-bye!"

"NOOO! Don't hang up!!" we all shouted desperately.

"Please, Brianna! Listen to me! Don't hang up!" I begged. "I was just calling to tell you that, um, you can play Princess Sugar Plum on my cell phone while we're sliding on the ice, okay?"

Long silence. "Really?"

"Really!"

"Goody gumdrops! Can Miss Penelope play too? I told her not to sneak your phone and play the Princess Sugar Plum game, but she did it anyway. It's all HER fault, not mine. But she's very sorry!"

"Sure, Brianna, Miss Penelope can play too."

"Okay! Thanks! BYE!"

"WAIT!!" I screamed. "I need to talk to Mom or Dad! It's an emergency."

"Daddy went to go get me popcorn. And Mom is talking to that lady from ballet class with the big mouth. I'm not supposed to interrupt Mom again, or else. But guess who I see walking by? It's BRANDON THE COOTIE GUY! Hi, Brandon the Cootie Guy! It's me! We talked on the phone, remember?! Nikki was in the shower and that dead squirrel was in Mrs. Wallabanger's backyard."

Muffled voices.

I could NOT believe Brianna was telling all of our personal business like that.

"Brianna! BRIANNA!" I yelled.

"WHAAAT!" she huffed.

"Can you give the phone to Brandon the Cootie

Guy? I need to talk to him. Okay?" I said.

"Well, just for a little bit. I'm supposed to be playing Princess Sugar Plum on this phone. Hold on."

More muffled voices.

"Hello, Nikki!"

"Brandon! OMG! We're stuck in a storage locker in the arena! Storage Area C, locker seventeen. Chloe's phone is about to die any minute. Please come get us out!"

"WHAT? Where did you say you were?"

"We're stuck in a—"

That's when the battery died on Chloe's phone and it went dead.

The three of us just sat there in the pitch-dark, stunned and speechless.

We had no idea whether or not Brandon had heard

any of the details about where we were. But just
when we were about to give up hope . . .

The show was starting in four minutes.

We raced back to our dressing room and grabbed our skates and clown wigs, with Brianna tagging along.

Her eyes lit up when she saw the huge, colorful gift-wrapped box. "Nikki, can I have that really big present?"

"No, Brianna, it's empty. That's just a prop for clowns to use."

"I wanna be a clown TOO!" She pouted.

That's when Chloe, Zoey, and I got the exact same idea at the exact same moment.

I guess the old saying "Brilliant minds think alike" is true.

The arena was filled to capacity, and the excitement was so electric you could feel it in the air.

Several local television stations were broadcasting live.

Victoria Steel, looking more glam than ever, warmly welcomed the audience and encouraged them to donate generously to the charitable organizations being represented in the show.

Then she made a surprise announcement. "To show our commitment to your community, in addition to the three thousand dollars that each organization is receiving, *Holiday on Ice* is going to award an additional ten-thousand-dollar cash prize to the crowd favorite."

At that news, the entire audience stood up and cheered like crazy.

Talk about crowd participation!

This was turning into *American Idol.*

On ICE!

The big cash prize sounded exciting and all. And I was sure Fuzzy Friends could use it.

But my personal goal was simply to try to get through the entire routine and perform well enough to be awarded the $3,000.

Soon the lights dimmed and the ice show got under way.

I wasn't the least bit surprised to see that MacKenzie had been selected as the opening act.

She skated to music from *Swan Lake* and was AWESOME!

And when she finished, the audience gave her a standing ovation.

As far as I could tell, MacKenzie was pretty much a major contender for the crowd favorite award. She knew it too, because she kept posing and waving to the audience. . . .

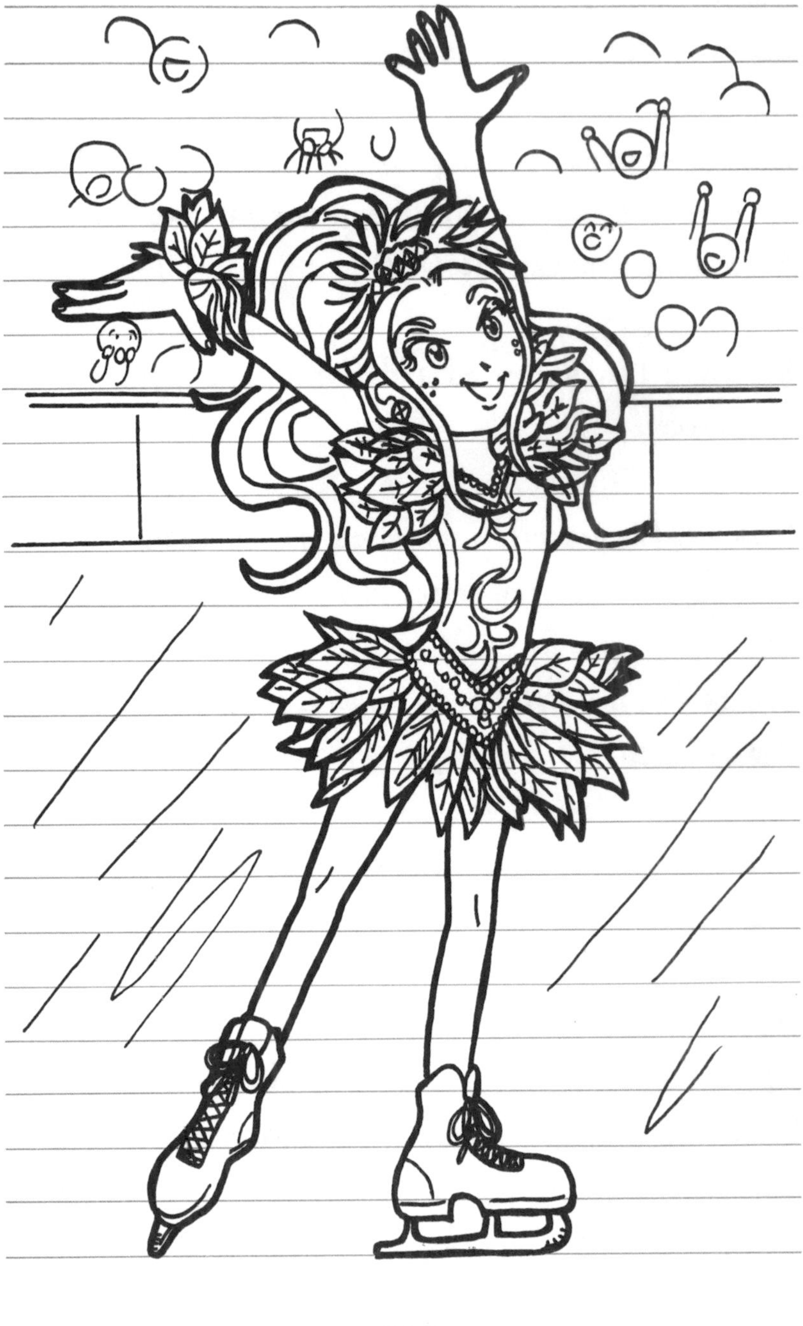

When MacKenzie came off the ice, she looked really shocked and surprised to see us in the waiting area backstage.

I smiled and waved, but she just stuck her nose in the air and walked right past us.

"MacKenzie, you're a rotten little sneak. That was a new LOW for you. You've obviously hit rock bottom and started to dig," I said right to her face.

She whipped around and sneered at me. "You say that like it's a bad thing. Actually, I was just trying to do you a favor by saving you and your little friends from public humiliation. But if you insist, go right ahead. LOSERS!"

By the time it was our turn to skate, I was a nervous wreck.

My knees were wobbly even BEFORE I got on the ice.

But somehow I made it into position without falling on my face.

As we waited for the music to start, Zoey gave Chloe and me a big smile.

Then she whispered loudly, "Every human being is a clown but only few have the courage to show it— Charlie Rivel."

I smiled. "Thanks, Zoey!"

OMG! The butterflies in my stomach were so bad I felt like I was going to lose my lunch right on the ice in front of the audience.

That's when Zoey whispered even louder. "A clown is an angel with a red nose—J. T. 'Bubba' Sikes."

I was like, "PUH-LEEZE! Enough already, Zoey. It was cute the first time, but the philosophical CLOWN-ISMS are starting to get on my last nerve!"

But I just said that inside my head, so no one heard it but me.

I knew she was just trying to make me feel better.

I was actually pretty lucky to have a BFF like her.

As the music blared over the speakers, Chloe and Zoey floated across the ice like graceful butterflies.

Okay. Like graceful butterflies wearing stupid clown costumes.

I was supposed to zig, but I zagged.

Or was I supposed to zag, but I zigged?

In any event, I tripped, fell on my butt, and slid across the ice at ninety miles per hour like a human bobsled.

Then, *BAM!!* I crashed right into the huge gift we were using as a prop.

Chloe and Zoey looked totally stunned and stopped skating.

I felt so terrible about messing up our routine, I wanted to cry. MacKenzie was right! All we were doing was making fools of ourselves.

I half expected to hear Victoria shriek,

"SECURITY! Get those CLOWNS off of my ice!"

And once we were kicked out of the show, Fuzzy Friends would close and Brandon would be forced to move.

I would probably never see him again ☹!

I just sat there stunned, too exhausted to get up.

But that's when I noticed the most amazing thing.

The entire audience was LAUGHING.

And all the little kids were on their feet pointing and clapping.

Apparently, they thought me skidding across the ice

on my behind and almost cracking open my skull was part of a little comedy act or something.

Then it occurred to me that we WERE wearing clown outfits.

DUH!

And clowns were supposed to be funny!

DUH!

And they were always falling on the ground and knocking each other over.

DUH!

I think Chloe and Zoey must have noticed the crowd's reaction and come to the exact same conclusion.

The crowd seemed to LOVE US!!

I mean, REALLY LOVE US!

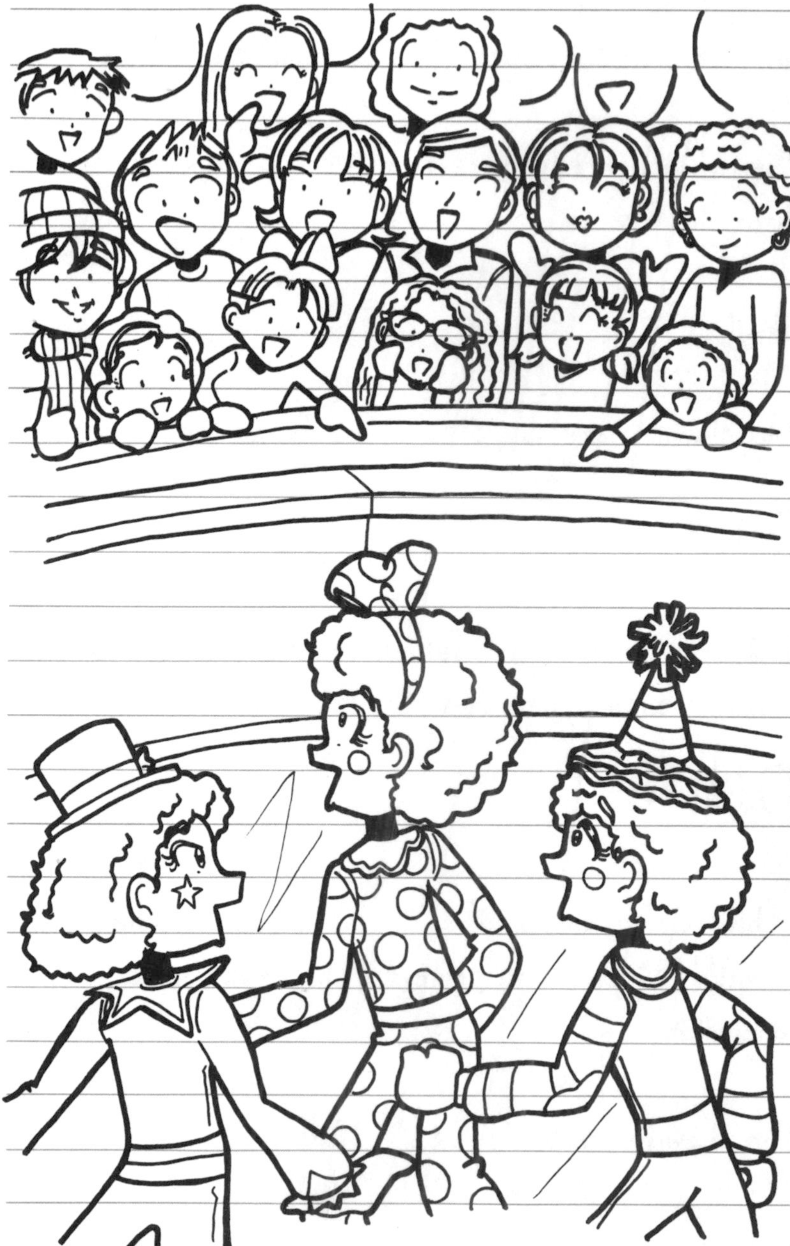

From that point on, we totally hammed it up.

The crowd went KA-RAY-ZEE when we started doing funky dance steps from our old *Ballet of the Zombies* routine. I'm guessing it was probably because no one had ever seen ZOMBIE CLOWNS do the MOONWALK in ICE SKATES before!

I even threw in a few dance moves from that time Brianna and I performed LIVE at Queasy Cheesy!

I felt so happy and relaxed that, suddenly, skating just wasn't that difficult for me anymore.

It almost seemed to come naturally.

FINALLY!

The strange thing was that I didn't accidentally fall down, not even ONCE, for the entire two and a half minutes that remained.

I only FELL DOWN on PURPOSE!

To make the crowd laugh.

Hey! I was a clown!

It was my JOB!

As our music ended I wanted to keep skating.

This was the most fun Chloe, Zoey, and I had ever had together.

But there's more!

The crowd got an unexpected surprise when a tiny little clown popped out like a demented jack-in-the-box. . . .

BRIANNA!!!...

I guess you could say she stole the show. . . .

ME, CHLOE, ZOEY, AND BRIANNA—
A SUPERCUTE CLOWN POSSE

We totally nailed that last pose, and the audience went WILD!! And we received a standing ovation.

After we got off the ice, we were SO happy! We did a group hug with Brianna and Miss Penelope!

I didn't think our day could get any better, but it did. Guess who won audience favorite and a check for $10,000 for Fuzzy Friends!

The whole time we were getting our picture taken, MacKenzie was glaring at me.

I wanted to walk up to her and say, "Hey, what's WRONG? You MAD, girlfriend? Huh? Is that it? You MAD?!!"

But I didn't. Because I was trying to be nice and show good sportsmanship.

In spite of the fact that SHE was the biggest CHEATER on the planet!!

I couldn't believe she stole our costumes AND locked us in that storage room.

But her evil little plan totally BACKFIRED on her.

CLOWNS knocking each other over and sliding around on their butts is really FUNNY stuff.

But prissy Sugar Plum Fairies doing the same thing? Not so much!

Just as I was coming off the ice, I saw Brandon, and he looked SO happy.

I almost DIED when he handed me a beautiful bouquet of flowers.

"Congratulations, Nikki!" Brandon said.

"Thanks, Brandon! This whole thing has been unbelievable."

"I heard there was a mix-up with your costumes too. But I knew you'd be okay. You guys totally rocked the ice!"

"Well, it was worth it. I'm just happy we were able to keep Fuzzy Friends open so that your gran—er, I mean Betty—can continue to take care of those animals," I said, and plastered a big, dopey grin across my face.

But deep down inside I cringed and wanted to kick myself for almost referring to Betty as Brandon's grandmother.

It's weird, but the better I've gotten to know him, the MORE questions I have about who he really is. And the LAST thing he needs right now is some busybody snooping into his personal business and gossiping behind his back.

I've personally lived through that with Miss Motormouth MacKenzie, and it's been TORTURE.

So for now, I know all I need to know—that Brandon is an AMAZING friend who's always there when I need him. And I'm happy I was able to be there for him too.

I hugged my bouquet of roses and buried my face in them.

I inhaled their sweet, romantic fragrance, awed by how much they smelled like perfumey . . . um . . . roses.

"Well, thank you for all your help. Nikki, you're . . . AWESOME!" Brandon gushed.

I blushed profusely.

Then he gave me a big hug!

OMG! I thought I was going to pee my pants.

BRANDON. ACTUALLY. HUGGED. ME!!

SQUEEEEEEE!!!

But now I'm even more CONFUSED!

Because I don't know if it was a . . .

"You're my FRIEND" hug.

Or a "You're my really GOOD friend" hug!

Or a "You're MORE than a good friend" hug!!

Or a "You're my GIRLFRIEND" hug!!!

I really want to ask him.

But I can't!

Because THEN he'll know . . .

I really want to KNOW!

And him knowing all of this would just make me
supernervous.

Which sounds really crazy.

Right?

Sorry, I can't help it.

I'M SUCH A DORK!!!
☺!!

Hey, you!

Wanna take a sneak peek at a few pages of my next diary, *Tales from a Not-So-Smart Miss Know-It-All?*

Shhhh! It's a secret. . . .

AAAAAHHHHH!!!

(That was me screaming!)

Right now I'm at Brandon's birthday party!

Locked in a bathroom!

Totally FREAKING out!

It all started earlier today when I got the WORST news EVER!

At the last minute my mom had to step in for a sick parent and be the driver for Brianna's dance class carpool.

Mom was all like, "Nikki, dear, I'm STILL planning to take you to Brandon's party. But we have a teeny-tiny complication regarding your transportation HOME. So your dad has agreed to help."

I could not believe my own mother would LIE right to my face like that. Sorry, Mom! But it WASN'T a teeny-tiny complication.

IT WAS A SUPERSIZED, GIGANTIC, HUMONGOUS BLOB OF A PROBLEM!!

WHY?

Because my parents casually informed me that I was going to be picked up by . . . wait for it, wait for it . . .

Dad and his very creepy, six-foot-long riding companion, MAX THE ROACH!

There was just NO WAY I was going to let everyone at Brandon's party see me getting into the roachmobile. Which, BTW, was STILL blinged out in tacky Christmas decorations.

Why couldn't DAD drive for Brianna's dance class?!

Then, instead of brutally traumatizing ME for LIFE, Dad could take Brianna and her little friends joyriding. It would be more fun than DISNEY WORLD!!

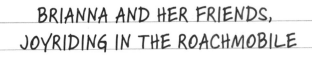

BRIANNA AND HER FRIENDS, JOYRIDING IN THE ROACHMOBILE

That's when I made a VERY difficult decision.

I was NOT going to Brandon's party ☹!

And being the honest person that I am, I planned
to tell Brandon and all my friends the truth:
Something had come up at the last minute.

Namely, my LUNCH! I was so SICK of my
life ☹!!

I had picked up the phone to break the bad news
to Chloe and Zoey when my mom knocked on my
bedroom door and stuck her head inside.

"Nikki, dear, would you please write down the time
you need to be picked up from your party along
with the address and telephone number and give it
to your dad? He doesn't have the best memory and
gets lost going to the mailbox."

Before I could tell her I'd changed my mind about
the whole party thing, she closed my door and
disappeared into the hall.

I just sighed and dialed Zoey's number.

Actually, Dad NOT finding the house would be a really GOOD thing because—

Suddenly a little lightbulb flashed on in my brain, and I had an idea that was pure genius.

Brandon's party was going to be at Theodore's house because he had a cool, arcade-style game room with an awesome sound system. The address was 725 Hidden Lake Drive. But what if Dad parked and waited for me about a block away?! At ANOTHER address? Then no one at the party would see me getting into the van with him and Santa Roach.

PROBLEM. SOLVED. ☺!!

I quickly hung up the phone.

Then I scribbled all of my party information for Dad.

Just like Mom had instructed.

Except I kind of fudged on the address-and-phone-number part:

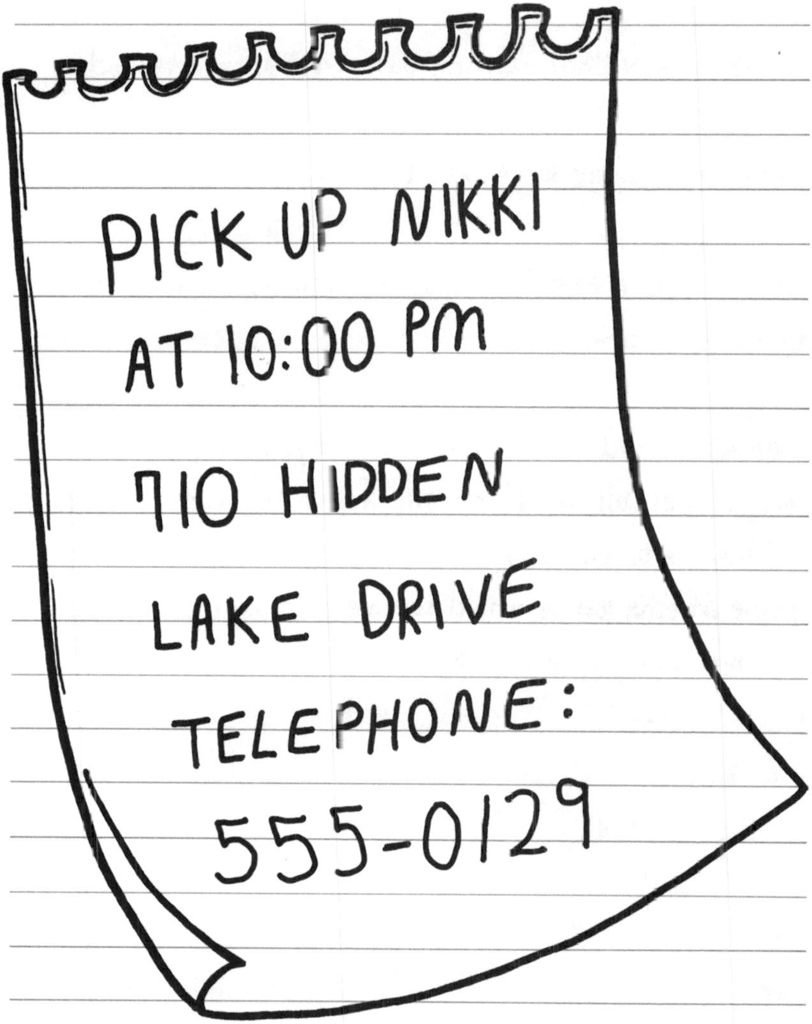
PICK UP NIKKI
AT 10:00 PM
710 HIDDEN
LAKE DRIVE
TELEPHONE:
555-0129

Was I not brilliant? ☺!!

Anyway, Brandon's party was just as fun as I had imagined.

It was really cool hanging out with all my friends.

Chloe and Zoey kept me laughing.

And Brandon and I talked to each other almost the entire time.

Theodore had just about every type of pizza imaginable delivered hot and fresh by Queasy Cheesy.

Yep—Queasy Cheesy!

I was shocked to find out that his family owns the one at the mall. As well as the other 173 locations in the national chain.

And get this! As a special treat, his dad gave each one of us three FREE gift certificates for an all-you-can-eat Queasy Cheesy Pizza Fest.

OMG! I was SUPERhappy about that!

Because if I gave one Queasy Cheesy certificate to Mom, one to Dad, and one to Brianna, I'd pretty much have ALL of my Christmas shopping done for next year!

Without having to spend ANY of my OWN money.

How COOL is THAT!

Anyway, I couldn't believe how quickly the time passed, and soon it was 10:00 p.m.

But we were having so much fun, no one wanted to leave.

I wasn't really the least bit worried because according to my brilliant plan, my dad was patiently waiting for me somewhere nearby.

So of course I had a complete MELTDOWN when the doorbell rang and . . .

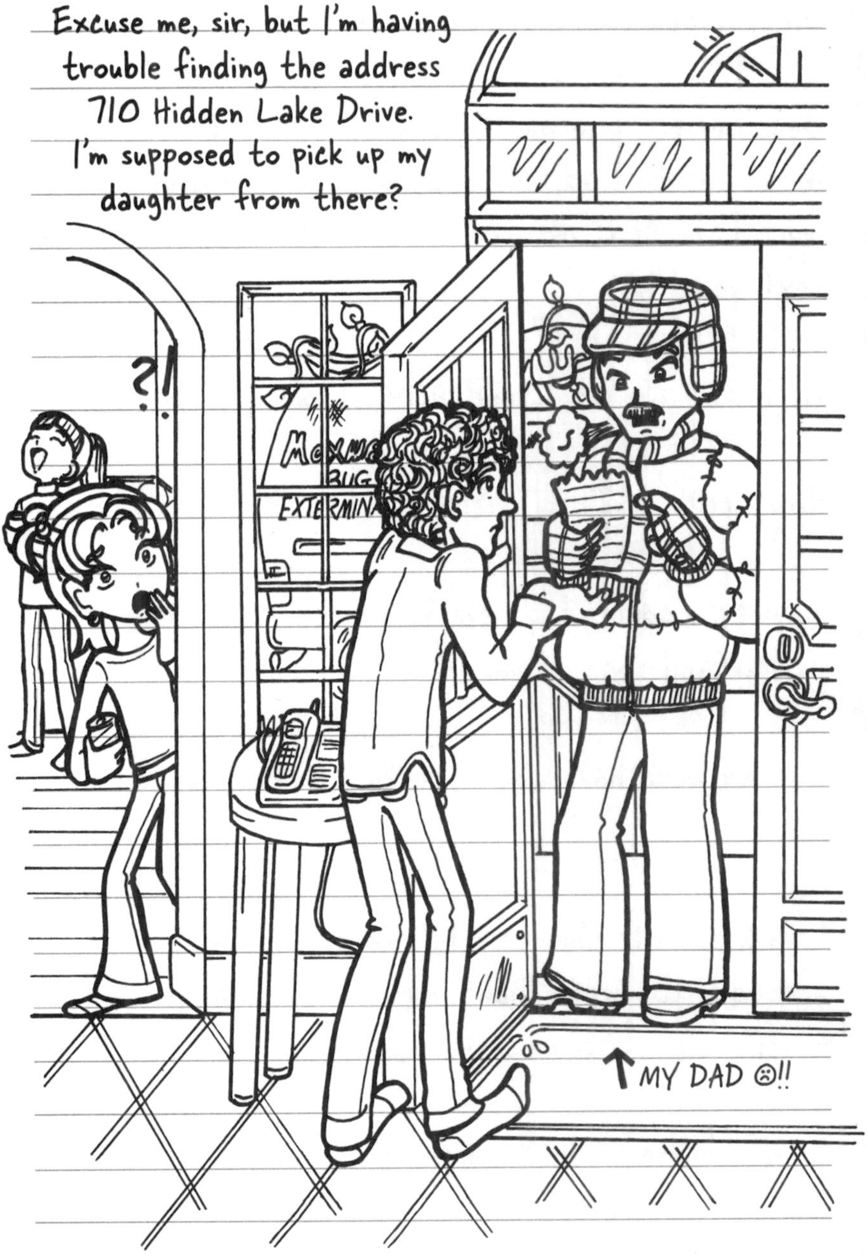
Excuse me, sir, but I'm having trouble finding the address 710 Hidden Lake Drive. I'm supposed to pick up my daughter from there?
?!
BUG
MY DAD ☹!!

OMG! MY DAD JUST CRASHED MY PARTY!!

AAAAAAHHHHHH!!!!

To be continued in _Dork Diaries 5: Tales from a Not-So-Smart Miss Know-It-All!!_ ☺!!

Rachel Renée Russell is an attorney
who prefers writing tween books to legal briefs.
(Mainly because books are a lot more fun and
pajamas and bunny slippers aren't allowed in court.)

She has raised two daughters and lived to tell
about it. Her hobbies include growing purple flowers
and doing totally useless crafts (like, for example,
making a microwave oven out of Popsicle sticks, glue,
and glitter). Rachel lives in northern Virginia with
a spoiled pet Yorkie who terrorizes her daily by
climbing on top of a computer cabinet and pelting
her with stuffed animals while she writes. And, yes,
Rachel considers herself a total Dork.